S

FLEMING, John Henry
The legend of the barefoot mailman

DATE DUE

34499

THE LEGEND

OF THE

BAREFOOT MAILMAN

The Legend of the Barefoot Mailman

A NOVEL

John Henry Fleming

Faber and Faber

BOSTON • LONDON

For Julie

First published in the United States in 1995 by Faber and Faber, Inc.,
50 Cross Street, Winchester, MA 01890.

Library of Congress Cataloging-in-Publication Data

Fleming, John Henry.
  The legend of the barefoot mailman : a novel / John Henry Fleming.
      p.   cm.
  ISBN 0-571-19879-1 (hardcover)
  I. Title.
  PS3556.L445L44   1996
  813'.54—dc20   95-21804
                                                            CIP

Jacket design by Jane Mjølsness

Printed in the United States of America

A NOTE FROM THE NARRATOR

THIS IS A STORY of fortune, which to my mind is not unlike a miscarried letter. It is passed from hand to hand, from mail carrier to mail carrier, from post office to post office in a desperate search for its rightful owner. Too often it remains undelivered, thanks to the postal service's lack of perseverance or the smeared and cryptic handwriting of the address. Sometimes it is delivered into the wrong hands, and then it may as well end up in the dead-letter box, since the fate of one man can do no good—indeed, may even do harm—to another. But then there is that happy circumstance where, usually by sheer good luck, such a package falls into the lap of its intended, and a man receives what is justly, what is poetically and smilingly, his. Here is the story of one such happy coincidence.

Prologue

I T BEGAN ON THE first day of an unusually hot summer in
the latter half of the previous century. A carrier for the
United States Postal Service walked the Florida beach route
between the Town of Biscayne (on Biscayne Bay) and the
Town of Figulus (on Lake Worth). The man was friend to no
one and acquaintance to few. There wasn't a soul within five
hundred miles who'd even know his name, and that was
probably for the best. It had been so long since he'd heard his
own name spoken that it is not impossible he'd forgotten it
himself.

Though not yet forty, the man was old before his time. Too
old, he knew, for what was surely the most strenuous mail
route in America—sixty miles each way on an empty, super-
heated beach, with nothing to break the monotony or ease the
pain.

He tottered achingly as he moved, falling forward to be
caught always at the last instant by his unsteady legs. His
hunched shoulders and overtanned skin seemed fixed in a
squint, as though his body had collapsed inward in some kind
of desperate, protective measure and now had the look of
something impenetrable that nevertheless would be beaten in
the end—by sheer persistence, by something as slow and constant as the sun. And if he were to meet a fellow traveler and

exchange a few words, the traveler would come away with a similar impression of the man's personality—bitter, self-reliant, and inevitably beaten.

But the carrier was unlikely to cross another's path here. South Florida was then still a frontier, and one that had been passed over by the hordes of westward-looking pioneers. Its beaches were empty but for the refuse of shipwrecks, its settlements few and far between, its native presence dwindling from years of brutal wars, deportation, and disease. This stretch of beach was lonelier and wilder than it had been in perhaps thousands of years, before the Spanish had built forts here to keep watch while they siphoned off the Fountain of Youth, and even before the natives had begun to clear land and plant their way into a short-lived prosperity.

The carrier would not find more than a few ghostly remnants of these civilizations: shards of a Spanish cannon sticking from the sand just far enough to stub his toes; or clumps of burial mounds fading like blemishes on the dense, flat coastal jungle.

Most of all the carrier would find heat. This day signaled only the beginning of summer's long and hellish reign, an endless succession of unbearable heat and humidity, enough to drive any man to delirium. His shirt was already drenched in sweat, though he dared not remove it and expose himself to the blistering sunlight. His pants were rolled above his ankles, starched by the sun, and jeweled with crystallized seawater. From time to time the lip of a swell would creep up the beach and soak his feet, but the water was too warm to provide much relief. And these feet, in any case, were being crucified by his shoes—the standard, government-issue, rubber-and-canvas carrier's shoes, not designed by any person familiar with the heat of a Florida summer.

The pain he felt in his feet had intensified through years of walking the beach, had gradually worked its way into his consciousness, and now threatened to occupy his every waking thought with itself and with its source: the shoes. As he walked in agony, he cursed the stupidity of the shoes' design, the way the material sponged up the water and heat, the way the low tops let in just enough dirt and grit to sandpaper his feet as he walked, and the way the buckles cut into the skin on his ankles if they were loosened enough to make the shoes fit properly. He imagined the committee of Yankee politicians who'd commissioned the design of the shoes, specifying the need to keep the postman's feet warm during the sleet, hail, and snow of a northern winter. He pictured the unveiling of the prototype before the committee some months later, and the politicians smiling approvingly and passing the shoe around as they comment on the uniqueness of the design and its pliable, one-size-fits-all material. Reporters ask them questions, pictures are taken with the politicians gathered behind the shoe as it sits on a pedestal in the middle of a huge oak table. Then one reporter suggests that someone try on the shoe, and the politician from New York volunteers laughingly as he curls one end of his waxed moustache and wedges a foot into the prototype. He is a fat politician, and the shoe doesn't fit him properly, though he smiles anyway. Everyone sees that the shoe is about to burst from the pressure of the politician's foot, but no one says anything, and the one-size-fits-all claim is carefully avoided for the rest of the press conference. For in reality, the shoes fit well only on a man whose feet are exactly average in every way. Average, that is, according to statistics compiled by a government committee.

This postal carrier's feet were not average by any measure. They were a basic ingredient of his lurching gait and a souvenir of his duty to the Confederacy. Early in the war, he'd done battle with a Union scouting balloon, running swiftly and fearlessly into harm's way when he saw it float into view above the Tennessee treetops. He'd leapt over bushes and torn his shoulders on the thorns and bark, firing with his rifle when the forest allowed him a glimpse of the sky. At last he broke into a meadow and saw that the balloon had begun to sink. He waited directly below it, imagining with great pride how he was going to take this Yankee back to camp, dead or alive. It was his first encounter with the enemy, and this victory was sure to mark him for a hero, was sure to lead to high praise and a rapid series of promotions and commendations.

The balloon fired up like an injured beast, sinking anyway, its roar sounding to him like little more than a death rattle. He smiled as he watched it grow, the basket like a neatly wrapped gift falling from the heavens into his open arms. He remembered his rifle then and turned his head down briefly to reload the barrel. When he heard a snap and looked up again, he saw the Yankee scout peering over his basket not more than sixty feet above and a sudden, disorienting upward motion to the balloon, though there wasn't time for his brain to register that fully. Later he'd remember, too, that in those few moments of heightened reality he'd also seen a knife in the scout's hand and a rope dangling over the side of the basket.

But at the time he saw only a blur of the sandbag that hit him, heard only the fuzzy crescendo of the cracking bones in his feet. And so crazed with pain was he that his first and only thought was a strange one indeed, that the scream he heard was coming from the sandbag itself and not from his open mouth.

He felt the pain all over again when the field doctor ordered the bag lifted from his feet. Unveiled before him were the flattened and misshapen dogs that would never fit properly into any pair of shoes again.

This was the incident that had embittered him for life and aged him prematurely. Rather than become the brunt of jokes and the object of pitying stares, he retired from the military and withdrew from society altogether, eventually landing this painful but solitary job with the postal service. He didn't care that a walking job was probably not the best line of work for a man with his condition; he could tolerate the physical pain so long as he was left alone with his bitterness, his self-pity, and his occasional drunken binges. He carried the mail all day

x

long in isolation, pacing himself so that he always arrived at his P.O. stops in the dead of night. That was an arrangement he'd made with the government man in St. Augustine who'd hired him: he'd never have to speak with a postmaster unless he chose to. Instead, he'd hang his sack of mail on the "Incoming" sign nailed to the back of the post office, he'd take a second sack off the "Outgoing" nail, and then he'd disappear into the hot, silent night.

So of course he blamed the government shoes for his pain, transferring his guilt and his self-loathing onto the generous dispensation of the conquerors who'd crippled him for life. Yet there was nothing he could do about it, because he could not afford or could not bring himself to purchase a more comfortable pair of shoes, and because the only alternative was to walk in his bare feet, which, under present conditions, would mean a slow, certain descent to the human limits of pain.

This frustrating knowledge now made him all the more angry. It intensified the pain and the heat and made the salty air sting like pin pricks on his cracked lips and his brittle lungs. It made the postal sack heavier until the strap seemed to gouge his neck and shoulders with every chafing step. It drove him to delirium and made him search for something— anything—that might serve as a better scapegoat and so provide some temporary relief.

To this end he stopped, trembling and out of breath, removed his sack and rifled through its contents, searching angrily for the heaviest offending package. He dug from the bottom one thick box, tidily wrapped in brown paper and twine and addressed to "Josef Steinmetz, Town of Figulus." He weighed it in his hands while he cursed its sender, its intended recipient, and the entire U.S. Postal Service for allowing such a heavy wrench to fall into the delicate machinery of mail delivery. All of his delirious anger and intense discomfort suddenly took a new shape. To him the box was monstrous and single-mindedly evil.

It had come from Brooklyn, and, like most mail out of the

North, by steamer to Key West, and then up to Biscayne on a little mail skiff. The journey could take anywhere from three weeks to three months, depending on the weather and the dispositions of its handlers. But this package, now only twenty miles from its destination, was about to take a long and scenic detour.

A drop of sweat fell into the carrier's eye, blinding him for a moment and finally sending him over the edge. He flew into an animal rage, leapt to his feet, cursing and holding the package above his head like some frenzied gorilla about to break the skull of its keeper. Then he ran down the beach and into the hot, slow surf, yelling something primal, and tossed the box as far as he could out into the mirrored waters, where it plunked below the surface, bobbed for a moment, and then began its drift out to sea.

"Goddamn Yankee rats," he said.

It was a futile lashing out at nature and fate, but for one brief, beautiful moment he felt a sense of power and relief.

Then the moment faded, and he continued in his agony, dragging himself slowly up the beach toward nightfall and the faceless little town of Figulus.

PART I

Serendipity

Chapter 1

THE FIRST SIGN came when Earl Shank pulled his face out of the shallows of Lake Worth and felt a sudden breeze brush across his salted lips. He'd begun the morning as he always did, waking up well after his wife and slipping out of the house while she fed the chickens. It was best for him to get over to the post office before she could invent something for him to do. He could check on whether his undependable mail carrier had shown up in the night with a new bag of mail. If not, he could always re-sort some mail, or re-check the figures in his accounts receivable ledger, or just wait around for someone to post a letter—at least until Mely showed up and told him there were better things he could be doing around the house. And then he'd say to her, "Mely, you jest don't understand. I got a responsibility to the nation. I got to guard against snags in the system." Then she'd give him that look, like his idleness was a sin against God and nature. And when he'd finally return to the house, she'd work all the harder just to punctuate her quiet argument. But by the time he felt the first pangs of guilt it'd surely be almost noon, and she'd have most of the chores out of the way.

Expecting the morning to run just like that, he'd started down the path that ran along the shore, where the strong morning sun had already made things quiet. The water moccasins had curled up in the weeds for the day. The gators had quit their yawning and moved off the banks to cool themselves in deeper waters. But there was something there—maybe even the hand of fate itself, he'd think later—that tripped him up and made him fall face first into the murky shallows, where he tasted the salty water and remembered his very first day here.

Twenty-two years ago, he'd clung to the side of a lifeboat whose oars smacked the ocean waves into his gasping mouth. There hadn't been room for him in that lifeboat, just as there hadn't been room for him in his family—he'd decided that just a few weeks earlier, when he'd left them to take a job on a trader. So when the waves had pressed in on him and the ocean reached out to make him one of her own, he'd resolved that his young life was a cursed failure and that it would probably be for the best if he let loose his grip and give himself freely to the depths. The moments in which he worked up the courage to do so were the most difficult of his life, but he finally threw his hands out and fell backward, closing his eyes, expecting the mildly annoyed face of his captain to be his last sight on this earth.

Instead, when his rear end hit the sandy bottom, he'd opened his eyes again and seen the first mate yelling at him to get off his lazy ass and help them beach the boat. He was just a few feet from shore. Cheated of even the brief solemn glory he'd expected in death, he no longer had the courage to try it again. So he obeyed the first mate's command and helped drag the boat across the strip of ocean beach. Then Earl clung to the boat again as the shipwrecked crew crossed Lake Worth to the little town the captain had heard of called Figulus.

They'd found then exactly what there was today: little overgrown paths branching away from the shoreline—paths so little used that one might easily mistake them for gator trails—and not a single house that could be seen by its closest neighbor through the trees. As they walked those little paths, they found no sign of human life—only houses that appeared to be deserted and a few hogs and chickens ambling around in the shade of the thick stands of palms. When they finally decided to push in the door of a house, they found a husband and wife in a cluttered and dusty room, moving almost imperceptibly in a pair of rocking chairs. The man looked up from the fish he'd been whittling out of a piece of driftwood, the woman from the Confederate flag she'd been crocheting to hang on their wall. But the entrance of sixteen men—some, like Earl, dripping wet—did not seem to disturb them in any way. That very fact had an instant and profound effect on Earl, who stood in the back, poking his head through the door. Those expressionless and ageless faces of indeterminate color struck him as a couple of perfectly blank slates, the kind of clean, smooth paper on which he'd only recently printed the publicity notices for his family's variety show. He smiled at them involuntarily, forgetting already his recent desire to end it all.

"What'll we do fer ya?" asked the man.

"We are shipwreck survivors of the SS *Seaworthy*," stated the captain, a hint of exasperation already showing in his voice, "and we would like some assistance in returning to our home port."

The man thought about this and rocked in his chair for a minute.

His wife said, "You ought to try ol' Jake. He's good at gettin around."

Her husband nodded in agreement.

"Down the path a stretch. Can't miss it."

The captain breathed an exasperated sigh, dumbfounded by the insignificance suddenly assigned to his shipwreck.

Then the men filed out after their captain, but Earl stayed behind and smiled again at those beautiful empty vessels smiling back at him from their rocking chairs. Since his job as ship's accountant for the *Seaworthy* had splintered itself on the reef offshore, he decided that his destiny lay elsewhere. Those faces and the raw and unexploited land had a

5

curious effect on him. He stepped outside and looked around, breathing in the ocean air and the fruits of the trees and the warm sunlight that bathed the land even in winter, and it all smelled to him like solid potential. He smelled a challenge for his natural publicity talents. He smelled his limitless future. He saw Florida for its inevitable becoming, and so he stuck his big foot in the door, determined to squeeze himself through to the other side, to the champagne and dainties he could practically taste when that warm breeze brushed across his salty lips.

AND THAT WAS the taste he remembered this morning, when a little breeze came out of nowhere and mixed with the salt water he was still spitting out of his mouth. It was the first sign that things were going to change, though he didn't recognize it yet. It wasn't until much later that he'd piece it all together. Then he'd think, *It was almost like somebody kicked me in the butt, jes so I could fall in an taste that water again, jes so I could wake up an smell my destiny.*

Because he'd forgotten it. And that was on purpose. Just as his neighbors tried to hide their houses in the trees, Earl had tried to hide the memory of his failures from himself. He'd given up on his fate, letting his life live itself. He didn't consider himself a lazy man, at least in his thoughts. His problem, he once told himself, was that his thoughts were too big for his body to know what to do with, though his body was by no measure small. But Florida had a history as a haven for good-for-nothing laggards who used laziness to their advantage—pirates and treasure seekers, wealthy retirees, pale convalescents, idlers rich and poor, con men and carpetbaggers, exploiters of people and ravagers of the land, entrepreneurs with big visions and flexible morals, anybody looking for a free lunch and a day in the sun. And though he wasn't schooled in the names and dates of history, Earl was sensitive to the attitudes and ideals of that long lineage, as though he were part of some old and venerated aristocracy whose values,

6

the usefulness of which was now long forgotten, would perpetuate themselves anyway, solely on the strength of history. Not that Earl fancied himself a prince, not even a prince of laggards. He was a man mediocre in every way. This he knew, and yet he'd always held his mediocrity itself in high regard. He'd counted it among his blessings. He'd used to believe that mediocrity, idleness, and a faith in the value of the imperfect were all a man needed for success. He'd used to think that that would be the moral of his autobiography, should the public demand he write one.

But for years now, he seemed to have lost his connection to the glory of that mediocrity. There'd been no easy success, no instant triumph for a wink in the right direction. He'd developed instead a personal history of failure and maybe a little too much effort for the tastes of his spiritual kin. That had beaten his confidence and his oversized scheming into a small, wistful pebble lost in the tired folds of his brain.

His first taste of failure came early in life, his real kin trying unsuccessfully to shape him in their own image. They were known as

——

THE SHANK FAMILY
VARIETY, DRAMA, AND ENTERTAINMENT REVIEW
Featuring Caleb and Cassandra Shank
—of noted Shakespearean fame—
AND INTRODUCING...
Those Adorable Shank Children,
Young Performers of Extraordinary Talent.

——

As Earl grew up on the stages of the small-town South, he performed his simple magic tricks, danced the little numbers choreographed by his mother, sang the adorable childish songs well into his teens, and juggled a few apples and oranges when one of his brothers was taken ill. But his magic tricks failed more often than not, his dancing was flat-footed and stumbling, and he hated singing and could never smooth the twang nor the adolescent cracks out of his voice. While his brothers and sisters developed bigger and bigger stage presences and joined their parents in more serious drama, Earl shied away, and his parents stopped encouraging him. The whole family understood that he simply did not have the talent to make it in theater.

Instead, at nineteen, he fell into the role of company bookkeeper and publicity manager. This he came to enjoy. He designed elaborate publicity notices, contacted the prominent citizens of each town, and generally got the word out while the rest of the family rehearsed. Then, with the show under way, he tallied the daily receipts, the bottom line of which he attributed solely to his hard work in the publicity department. He took the greatest pride in this, and soon knew that he had a natural talent for it. With publicity, he thought, he could provide great opportunities for himself and his family. He worked up grand schemes for highly publicized world tours and hitherto unheard of variety stunts, like "Shakespeare Performed atop Camels—Those Odd and Mysterious Ships of the Desert," or "Bring-Your-Own Snake Wrasslin." But when he brought these ideas to the attention of his family, they could only laugh. They treated his ideas as childish fancies and saw his role in the family business as inartistic drudgery, which they were only too happy to leave to the less talented. In their eyes, Earl would always be the failed artist. It wasn't long before he felt this and knew that he was underappreciated, and would be as long as he remained with his family.

So one night, concluding sadly that his destiny lay elsewhere, he packed a small bag of clothes, leaving all his childhood costumes behind, and stole away with only a brief note of explanation:

Family,
    Leaving to seek my fortune. The books and money (less my wages) are in trunk by my bed $\longrightarrow$
    Y'alls acting talents never rubbed off on me, but I think I got a talent for publicity. So there's my future for you. Sorry for the trouble I'll cause.
    Great Adoration,
    Your Lone Stray Son Earl

It was 1861, and with the war between the states fast approaching, Earl walked to Savannah and took that fateful job on the SS *Seaworthy*, a Caribbean trader, hoping eventually to work his way off the ship and into the main office up in Charleston, where he could make his publicity skills pay off. When the *Seaworthy* foundered on the reef just a few days later, he was certain his young life was cursed. But those beautiful empty faces and that salty breeze awakened something boundless and exhilarating within him. So when the crew finally found a guide to walk them the day and a half north to the new Jupiter lighthouse, where they could signal a passing ship, Earl remained behind. "Y'all go on ahead," he said, martyr-like. "I sorter like it here."

It was an easy decision for him. The only satisfying moments of his life had come when he'd seen those crowds pour in for his family's variety shows and he could sit back in the door of his family's tent and total the receipts, knowing it was all his doing, all thanks to his publicity skills. Of course those moments were tinged with pain, too, because his family had already branded him a loser. But now he had a chance to recreate his satisfaction on the grandest of scales. He would create fame and fortune where none had existed before. He would create a thing of beauty from the ground up. Then he could watch those crowds pour in and those receipts pile up bigger than his family would ever have imagined possible. And in a town like this, the credit would have nowhere to fall but on him.

Earl's big ideas made the town a little fidgety at first. They were a collection of loners and stragglers, all hiding from something—the law, or civilization, or conscription in the Confederate Army. Since they'd all come here to get away from people in the first place, these boatloads of tourists and new settlers Earl talked about would bring the risk of the pasts they'd left behind. But the settlers of Figulus had two traits in common, if nothing more: they were not disposed to dwell on the future, and they avoided trouble and conflict at all costs. These were exactly the qualities that had brought them here, after all. So the idea that the area could ever become a tourist haven sounded so preposterous to them, and this newcomer came across as such a wide-eyed goof, that in the end they chuckled the whole thing away and let Earl go about his business without interference.

His first great idea was to get the town incorporated and make himself postmaster. Then, he thought, he'd be in touch with a vast network of cheap publicity. And since the town had no governing body, he'd be its only official and could act by default as its representative. He'd be the conduit between Figulus and the outside world, and the destiny of the town would lie in his hands.

When he sent a letter to the Postmaster General's office up in Washington, he was told in reply (some four months later) that the town would have to have a minimum of fifty residents to qualify for a post office. So began Earl's first publicity campaign. He spent his last ten dollars at the print shop in Fort Pierce, making flyers and sending them to post offices in all the major Florida settlements:

—

SETTLERS WANTED
To Incorporate the Beautiful, Bounteous
TOWN OF FIGULUS
Located on the peaceful shore of Lake Worth,
Along Major Trade Routes,

With Plans in the Works for

A MAJOR SHIPPING PORT,

and UNTOLD NATURAL RICHES

Available to all Residents

—FAMILIES, LONERS, NATURE-LOVERS, AND ALL HONEST,
HARD-WORKING MEN AND WOMEN

WANTED IMMEDIATELY.

Paid for by Earl K. Shank,
POSTMASTER-ELECT.

———

The settlers came, mostly of the loner variety. Some left immediately when Earl could not produce the plans for a shipping port. The ones who stayed made the original settlers uneasy again, and they were uneasier still about Earl, whose ridiculous plans were beginning to work, and who seemed to want eventually to make their sleepy town into a home away from home for rich old Yankees. But as always, the town's cowardly nature shone through. No one could complain when they got approval for their post office. "I reckon that's what he's really after," they said as they hammered together the driftwood walls of the new post office building. "A good job with the government." Because they all were downtrodden or in hiding, they could appreciate a young man's efforts to get ahead. So they simply withdrew into their homes and stayed away from the newcomers.

The success of this first action filled Earl with great confidence, and he began to implement the next phase of his plan—to attract some major business interests to build a small port and trade with the locals. The shipping and trading companies would provide an astronomical boost to the local economy, and then he could begin to prepare the town for tourists by building hotels, restaurants, and theaters; such a setup would be certain to attract the up-and-coming pleasure-cruise industry, and then Figulus and Earl Shank would be well on their way.

So he encouraged the local small farmers to begin planting their citrus crops in huge quantities, and the local fishermen to gear up their boats for a commercial fishing industry, and the local trappers to stock up on alligator hides, because they were all going to get rich when the trading companies opened for business.

And then nothing happened. The trading companies did not want to invest in an unproven area and its evasive local population. Few companies bothered even to respond to Earl's inquiries, and several trips north to Fort Pierce and south to Biscayne netted him nothing but sore feet and closed doors. Things began to go terribly wrong. Slowly, the settlers he'd attracted began to slip away. Some of them made excuses at first, but eventually they told Earl right to his face, "You done us wrong, Shank. There ain't nothing here but a jungle full of skeeters, and there ain't likely to ever be anything else." They shook their heads. They spat on the ground. Then they packed their few belongings and left, most of them back up the coast, looking for any small town with a street and a few horses, maybe some single women. Quickly the town dwindled from fifty-three to the twenty-two original residents.

These events began to take their toll on Earl. He tried bigger and bigger schemes and made bigger and bigger claims about the town, as though each failure necessitated an even bigger success to undo the injury. The Fountain of Youth Spa attracted some interest for a while, until he was caught filling the little waterhole with decidedly unhealthful and unrestorative swamp water. He never got more than a few cypress trees cut for the five-hundred-room Lazy Palms Resort. The president never turned up at the Presidential Vacation Retreat, despite Earl's repeated invitations. And the organizers of the World's Fair declined even to respond to his letters, despite the sketches he sent them of the "nearly complete" Exposition Center.

Within a few years, when all his plans and his invitations and inquiries were responded to only with silence, Earl was

reduced to desperation. He felt cursed again, and the townsfolk reinforced this notion, peering out of their windows with
fright as he walked up and down the paths in a fidgety sweat.
He couldn't stand the sight of those blank faces he'd once
thought so beautiful, so he started spending his days at the
beach, where he jumped and waved at freighters as they
passed, hoping to bring someone—anyone—ashore, to show
them the town, how beautiful it was and how rich with possibility if only a few investors had a little foresight. He did suc-
ceed once. A small trading ship anchored offshore and a small
group of the crew paddled in, thinking Earl was a shipwreck
survivor. When they found the truth, Earl waving his arms
and ranting about natural riches and honest working folk and
inlets and harbors, the sailors became enraged and pummeled
Earl to the sand, then buried him up to his neck. It took a couple of concerned townsfolk to travel out to the beach and locate Earl's mosquito-bitten, delirious head and drag him back
to his little shack behind the post office, where they splashed
cool water on his sunburned cheeks, saying, "You're a lucky
man, young Shank, a right lucky man."

He remembered those words against his will this morning
as he brushed the mud and grass off the front of his overalls,
and the memory brought back all the pain and regret of the
failures he'd tried to suppress. It was as if the ghost of his past
had taken on a life of its own and now was going to follow him
around and, when he least expected it, trip him up and push
him in the mud, then whisper those painful words in his ear—
"You're a lucky man." It wasn't until much later, when he'd
put it all together, that he understood the ghost was really
only his bruised and bitter imagination feeding dark sarcasm
into places it didn't belong. Because neither the first time they
were uttered by the well-meaning townsfolk nor this morning, when they were whispered to him by what he'd later
know was fate itself, did those words have any meaning but
God's Honest Truth.

He shook the water out of his old shoes and kept down the path toward the post office, the taste of that breeze still on his lips. He knew the U.S. Government would be appalled at him manning his post in these muddy clothes. But he'd done so well in slipping out behind Mely's back that it would be a shame to ruin that now. He would need these morning hours to himself to overcome the painful memories that had been forced upon him. And work—at least Mely's kind—would not make him forget.

Mely was a good woman who'd softened the blow of his failures, but she seemed to want to make him atone for them through hard labor. They'd married just five years ago, when Earl was thirty-six. Old Jake Morris was her first husband; when he'd drowned in a fishing accident out on the lake, he'd left poor Mely a lonely widow. She was known by everyone as the best cook in town, and more than likely the best in the whole state of Florida, but Earl had never once tried her alligator stew or her coconut cream pie. That all changed when he decided he'd played the sad and lonely bachelor for too long, and that if he was ever going to have satisfaction in his life, he ought to find himself a good, solid woman. That was Mely, certain enough—a strong, thick Southern Country Woman. Though she was six years his senior, he began to call on her anyway after waiting five weeks, which he calculated as a proper grieving period for a guy like Jake.

Earl and Mely got along fine, and even better when he tasted her coconut pie. One bite, and some of the old fire at last came back to him. He was in love, and he looked deep into her cool brown eyes and a word popped into his head that would one day change his life: "restaurant."

He didn't tell her the plans until after they were married at the judge's chambers in St. Augustine. On their wedding night at the Augustine Inn, he asked her if she'd ever thought about cooking professionally.

"I ain't that kind of girl," she said in that matter-of-fact tone she used with all men.

"That ain't what I mean, hon," said Earl. "I'm talking chefs, restaurants, maitre d's, that sort of thing."

She was amenable to the idea. She admitted that she'd had a dream about it once.

Two days later, when they returned to Figulus, Earl started work on the restaurant. The newlyweds moved into Mely's house, which was bigger and more comfortable than Earl's, and Earl used the wood from his old shack to make the restaurant an addition to his new home. They'd start small, he thought, a seating capacity of maybe twenty, but eventually the restaurant would be known throughout Florida—just Florida, because Earl was getting older now, and he couldn't think any bigger than that, especially after his previous experiences.

Two months later, Earl and Mely's was open for business. The locals came out of respect for Mely's cooking, but they weren't rich and couldn't afford to eat out much. Everyone soon realized that this was just another of Earl's schemes doomed to failure. Earl sent out flyers to other communities up and down the coast, but there wasn't a meal in this world good enough to make someone sail for three days in unpredictable weather to a small town in the middle of nowhere.

After a few long months of empty tables and food that had to be given away because it was spoiling, the restaurant opened its doors only on demand, and then the guests usually brought their own food for Mely to cook. A small fee was charged then, and a little profit made. But for Earl, the money wasn't the thing.

Once again, his plans had gone sour, and it felt like the final blow. He had to resign himself to a small, comfortable life with Mely, a fine woman who worked just a bit too much. He kept the restaurant open one night a week for a time, but eventually closed it for good because it only served to remind him of his failure.

From that time until this very morning, he'd worked mainly on his forgetting. He'd done a fine job, he saw now, so fine that he'd no longer remembered he had anything to forget. That's why, when it came back to him like this all at once, it hurt more than ever.

THE POST OFFICE was located just beside the town's little dock. It was nothing more than a shack made from the salvage of a shipwreck. Some of the planks of wood were rotted out, so after a hard rain they'd stay waterlogged and creak noisily for several days, as though reliving the gale that had split them apart and washed them ashore. Earl walked around back and was happy to find a mail sack hanging from the Incoming nail. Now he'd have an excuse if Mely came to fetch him.

The sack was especially light this week, he thought. Couldn't be more than eight or ten letters and maybe a few packages, none of them big. He pushed in the fine-looking door that had probably once been the entrance to a captain's quarters. The place was well-enough lit, especially in the morning, from the light that poured in through the porthole he had for a window, through the door that he always kept open during business hours, and through the many chinks in the misaligned driftwood planks. On one end of the table he used for his mail sorting and for his business with customers there were the eighteen boxes stacked three high where the residents of Figulus claimed their mail. By Earl's count there were now twenty-seven residents at any one time, give or take a few comings and goings no one had noticed yet. He emptied the contents of the mail sack on the other end of the table. Then he pulled up his stool and slumped his chin onto his hand so that his wet belly pushed up against the table's edge. He leaned forward just slightly to pass a little gas, and then began to sort through the mail, trying not to think about the pool of regret that had seeped into his vision, trying to forget again what he'd worked so hard to forget these past few years, and cursing the salt water and the breeze he should have seen as the first sign of his reawakening. He hadn't yet noticed the image that had just appeared in his doorway like an apparition. But when he did, he would see that dark little man framed in the sacred light of a summer morning, immobile and waiting for recognition, and much later, he'd recognize it clearly as the second sign.

Chapter 2

JOSEF STEINMETZ STOOD in the open door of the post office
and paused to give his eyes time to adjust. He'd planned it
this way—a single, confident stride through the door and then
a pause. But now he regretted it. He'd really done it so as not
to seem overanxious—there was something indecent, he'd always thought, about people in a rush to retrieve their mail.
But this was too much. The pause was far too dramatic. Now
he felt planted on this spot and couldn't think of a graceful
way to overcome his inertia. He'd wanted so much to make a
good first impression on his fellow pioneers and already he'd
blundered with his first step into their midst. When the postmaster looked up from his duties, he'd surely laugh at the buf-
foonish sight in his doorway. It occurred to Josef that it might
be better to leave now before the postmaster even saw him.
He could return another day and begin again without this ill-
conceived hesitation. But what would he say to his wife? It
was in her honor he'd made this trip into town. To tell her the
truth would make him a coward and a fool in her eyes. To tell
her a lie would make him the same in his own eyes. Not only
had his little pause made him into a melodramatic fool, it had
trapped him in a checkmate.

Though he'd been here nearly ten weeks, this morning was
his first trip into town. Prior to this day, he hadn't considered

himself worthy enough to be called a citizen, and thus felt he had no business speaking with other residents, much less retrieving his mail. But this day was special to him. Not because his house was complete—that had been accomplished six weeks ago. Not because his citrus grove had sprouted— happily, he'd seen the first budding even before he'd put the finishing touches on the house. Not because Lena had finally joined him in their new home—he'd retrieved her from the port in Biscayne ten days ago. But because today was the first day he'd been able to convince her to leave the house and work with him in the grove. Though he didn't know it, it was also to be the last.

For two months, he'd slept in a canvas hammock, working on his house in the mornings and tending to his budding cit rus grove in the afternoon. Only when the young trees looked green and firm enough to survive did he send for his bride, Helena. She was the woman he'd shared all his dreams with and the one he wanted there with him when those dreams took shape and became ripe for picking. But he hadn't ex- pected her enthusiasm to wither so quickly.

The boat ride up from Biscayne had been a horrifying expe- rience for her. Josef paddled up the coast by river and ocean while Lena tried to shield herself from the constant rain- storms. The storms hadn't been heavy and the seas hadn't been dangerous, but Lena was unprepared for even that much expo- sure. She shivered, though the temperature was at least eighty degrees. She began to cry, too, and pleaded with Josef to take her home, though she knew full well that they were headed for home—their new home. When Josef tried his best to comfort her and allay her fears, she became still more frightened and angry and stopped just short of cursing him. Josef trembled at the strength of her reaction. It was a side of Lena he had never seen back in Brooklyn, and her rejection of their new home felt to him like a rejection of their marriage vows.

Lena, like Josef, was an immigrant from the Old Country who'd then lived most of her life in Brooklyn. But somehow

19

she'd become more citified than Josef, and she wasn't adapting well to the tropics—to a place without theaters, or great marketplaces, or fashionable shops and broad avenues. She'd collected herself and said nothing more since she'd arrived at Figulus, but Josef could see the way she looked at him while the bugs swirled around her head—her squinting eyes, her pouting lips. He'd hoped she would share the excitement of the grove and help him tend to the oranges and grapefruits. He'd hoped that they would become partners in the field the way they were partners in life. That was how he remembered husbands and wives in the Old Country. But, so far, it hadn't worked that way.

Still, while Lena had sat indoors these first nine days, Josef remained hopeful and continued to make plans. As his trees matured, he thought, he'd plant even more, and eventually he'd need to hire men to help him harvest. He hoped to make Figulus the regular stop of one of the growing number of freighters that passed by out in the Gulf Stream, freighters now laden with tropical fruits from the huge Caribbean plantations. One day, he thought, his fruits would be sold in the street markets of Brooklyn, where his Aunt Lois and his Uncle Mordy could pick them up and taste their sweet, exotic flavor. Nothing would make him prouder.

Then just this morning, Lena stopped him on his way out to the grove, held his arm and asked if she might come with him. "The beasts there can't be much worse than they are in the house," she said flippantly. But Josef was sure she knew how much this meant to him, and he smiled at her courage and her willingness to please him. He kissed her between the eyes and led her out to their burgeoning little grove. When he'd showed her its progress and instructed her in certain aspects of its care, he handed her the hoe, took a deep breath of the dewy morning air, and announced, "Lena, today I will go into town and announce our presence in the area. I'll secure for us a box at the post office and receive the postal well-wishes of our relatives in Brooklyn. Because today not only are we man and wife in the eyes of God and the law, we are man and wife in the eyes of our fellow pioneers. We're now a team, working for progress and the betterment of mankind."

It was the proudest moment yet in Josef's young life. And his eyes were so glazed with pride that he didn't see the look of distress on Lena's face nor the awkward way she held the hoe in her fingertips, as though she were disdainful of even touching such an unpleasant implement.

This proud feeling had stayed with him all through the morning to this very moment when he stood inside the post office door, shamed into immobility by the drama of his own entrance.

AFTER A FEW TENSE moments, the postmaster finally looked up from his mail sorting, and this gave Josef the impetus to move out of the light. He didn't notice the postmaster's dirty wet overalls or the curious way he was looking at him. He regretted later that he was so nervous and out of sorts that he didn't even wait for the postmaster to address him.

"My name is Josef Steinmetz," he blurted in his not fully suppressed Austrian accent, "and I would like to receive my mail."

The postmaster looked him over and gave him a strange smile, which Josef read as a clear indication of his own impropriety.

"Wellsir, lemme just see here." After a few thankfully brief moments, he held up an envelope. "Wouldn't ya know."

Josef took it from him. Then, anxious to remove himself from a disaster of his own making, he quickly nodded his head and backed his way out into the hot morning.

JOSEF ROWED BACK across Lake Worth to his little house on the opposite shore, replaying the events of this first meeting with the postmaster. He hadn't made the impression he'd wanted. Perhaps the man had overlooked the foolish dramatics of his entrance. But he couldn't have missed the stumbling way he'd approached the counter. And then he'd rushed right into asking for his mail. That was all wrong, he saw now. He should have made small talk. He should have brought up the latest advancements in horticulture or inquired about the weather patterns this time of year. Instead, he'd fallen into the trap of the overanxious postal customer. Why, he'd practically yanked the letter out of the postmaster's steady grip. That was the kind of *faux pas* to start rumors, to turn his fellow pioneers against him. He'd have to be more careful.

He'd built his house on this thin strip of land between Lake Worth and the Atlantic Ocean, a short canoe's ride from the town proper of Figulus. Like other houses in the area, it was pieced together with driftwood from shipwrecks—always abundant from the nearby beach—and its roof was thatched with palmetto leaves. It was somewhat cruder than most, owing to his determination to do the job himself, even though he had little experience in carpentry. There were embarrassing cracks in the walls where bugs and rain would enter uninvited, and every now and then a piece of the roof would fall in, bringing with it the scurry of a half dozen cockroaches and small snakes who'd made their homes up there. Such an event would also send his wife scurrying, to a corner of the room where she trembled and cried out in squeaks and gasps until the beasts had been removed or destroyed.

Still, he *had* built the house himself, and he considered it to be one of the greatest accomplishments of his young life— he was just twenty-four.

As he stepped onto the porch he called to his wife and got no answer. *Ah*, he thought, *she's probably hard at work in the grove*. This idea improved his attitude greatly, and he suddenly remembered the letter he'd held in his hand all the way across the lake. He'd crumpled it against the handle of his oar, and now sat down and straightened it out to read. He saw by the handwriting that it was from his Aunt Lois.

As he read, his face contorted in a mixture of sadness and pain. He'd plucked it so quickly and innocently from the postmaster's hand, unaware that its words would change him forever.

June 3

My Dearest Josef,

It is my sad duty to bear the news that your Uncle Mordecai has passed on. He left us quietly, his favorite pipe, filled with his favorite tobacco, still dangling from his mouth when I tried to rouse him. I have no last words to report. He'd had some breathing problems, and Doctor Fremdlich said he'd likely taken in some air that didn't agree with his constitution. We will miss him always.

I am pleased that Mordy was able to send off your birthday present before he was taken from us. I hope you are getting some use out of the loafers. Mordy picked them from the finest shop in all of Brooklyn, and they are made of the finest leather, imported from the Old Country. He did not want you to forget the craftsmanship of your forefathers, nor the grand style of the American city you once called home. Give my love to Lena.

With Fondest Affection,

Your Aunt Lois

In this moment, all the good feeling was drained from his body, and he wept quietly and for a long time on the step of the porch. His Uncle Mordy was the man who'd raised him like a son. He was the man who'd nurtured him and taught him the ways of the New World. For the first time, Josef realized that everything he'd done since he was old enough to do anything worthwhile, and most of all what he'd accomplished so far in his new home and what he hoped to accomplish as a pioneer, had been with a mind to pleasing Mordy. Mordy had always been there over Josef's shoulder, smiling on him, guiding him, the supreme earthly judge of his actions. Now, suddenly, he was gone.

The air had grown still and heavy and the mosquitoes had begun to swarm. Josef collected himself a moment, struck a match and lit the smudgepots around the house. Then, trembling, he looked at the letter again, staring at the words but unable to read them, thinking, *What are these shoes she speaks of? Why did I not receive them?*

JOSEF, LIKE HIS father, and his father before him, and all the men in his patrilineage that anyone could ever remember, had been born in the town of Melk, on the great Donau River. There was a convent there where the nuns made the finest wine in all of Austria, and for as long as anyone could remember, Josef's family had held the exclusive right to sell that wine, through a small retail shop in town, and also in larger quantities up and down the Donau. Josef's fondest memory of Austria was the warm feeling of his family gathered around a huge tub of wine bottles, pulling them out one by one and labeling them with the fancy labels designed by his Uncle Mordy—"MelkWein" in tall, fancy script, and in the background, a beautiful rendering of a convent on a cliff, the river running below it. It was a beautiful scene to look at, even though the convent on the label looked nothing like the real convent. Not that the real convent was ugly, but it wasn't the kind of convent to grace a wine label. It was a long, low, barn-shaped building made of ancient stones, sitting in a grassy field—a nice field, always meticulously groomed and smelling of all kinds of wonderful flowers in spring, but a field just the same—not the majestic, craggy cliff in the rendering, with its treacherous path winding up from the river. The few times that Josef went out to the convent when his father had business there, he could not even see the river from it. He could look out across the long, low field and see in the distance a great old castle that stood above a bend in the river. *Maybe this is Uncle Mordy's model for the fancy label*, he thought. Still, the castle looked nothing like a convent.

When Josef was only six, his world was shattered by a mysterious chain of events that he felt ought to have little to do with him. His father explained that in a far off country, a man called Pope had died, and a new man was chosen to replace him. He, too, was called Pope. This new man had new ideas, and issued orders that, interpreted by men in Austria, became rules requiring the nuns to stop manufacturing their wine.

That was all it took to ruin the Steinmetz family. Josef's father had no other skills, and in such a small town as Melk there were few opportunities, particularly for a man well into his forties. For a time, they tried to make their own wine, having transplanted some of the nuns' vineyard into their own little backyard. They bottled it and sold it under the old name, but the taste was not so good, and some jealous neighbor started a rumor that the new wine might cause corns.

In debt and despairing, Josef's father gathered the children together in the room they used to label the wine. He told them tearfully that circumstances had forced him into some terrible decisions, and now their little family, like their business, would have to be dissolved. Josef's mother broke into desperate, defiant sobs and tried to run out the door, screaming that she would rather leave now than see all her children sent away. But his father stopped her with his strong arms and held her close, squeezing her shoulders and calming her the way he always did, making the whole family believe that things would be all right, though for most of them the feeling was short-lived.

They were all to be sent to relatives, some near and some far. Josef, who even at his young age had shown himself to be intelligent and industrious, though not overly robust, was to travel by ship to Brooklyn, to be delivered to Uncle Mordy and Aunt Lois, who only two years before had kissed the whole family goodbye, thinking perhaps forever, and left for America.

This surprise delivery filled Mordy and Lois with delight. They loved children, though they'd been unable to have any themselves, owing to a condition in Mordy that Josef's father had always called "weak sperm." They accepted Josef and raised him as their own, thanking the heavens daily for the gift they'd always dreamed of. But Josef thought they ought to be thanking Pope.

Josef grew up a city boy, then—a New World boy, his uncle called him—though he never forgot his heritage, and always pledged to return home and care for his parents in their old age. He did well in school, excelling in mathematics and geography, and worked after hours in Mordy's print shop, where Mordy was training him to take over the business. But Josef's ideas about his future changed suddenly when, within a year of his fourteenth birthday, both his parents died. They'd grown old rapidly after the children left, and though Mordy had sent them what he could out of his modest profits, it was only enough to keep them out of debtor's prison. They died alone, broken-hearted and broke.

In his youthful frustration, Josef put the blame on his father. He was the one who'd said everything would turn out all right, and Josef had believed him, had been the only one to believe constantly and unquestioningly in him. All those years, Josef had believed that one day his family would be reunited, that his father would once more gather them in with his strong arms and hold them there forever, to bottle the wine and paste on the labels the way they used to. Josef saw now that it had all been an illusion, like the beautiful scenery on their fancy wine labels. His father hadn't cared about the truth; he'd cared only about a sales pitch. Even when he'd known there was no truth in what he sold, he'd insisted—out of pride, or fear, or just selfish habit—on selling it anyway. The real truth, thought Josef, was that his father's arms had grown too weak to hold his wife and children. Finally they'd grown so weak that he couldn't even hold himself. It was a pathetic picture, and one that made Josef angry. He'd been duped, after all, by the man he'd loved and venerated unconditionally.

With the death of his parents, then, Josef felt his ropes to the Old World cut all at once. He had to get as far away from that world as possible. He now had something to prove, and his young mind drifted through his difficult years, sometimes exuberant with possibility, sometimes lost and despairing, but finally settling in the big sky of American opportunity. He loved and respected his adopted parents more than ever, and perhaps the great love he showed for Mordy was partly a reaction to what he'd concluded about his father, partly a need to attach himself firmly to his life in America. And partly it was a human need for a smiling face over his shoulder—a new set of big arms—though he would never have admitted it then.

It was during this time that he realized Mordy's print shop, though increasingly successful, wasn't going to be enough for him, and he decided to become a pioneer, like the great nameless men and women he'd read about in his geography books. As soon as he was old enough, he would set out to carve his name in the finest old tree of the American wilderness.

When he met the young Miss Helena Lenosha, he knew he'd be carving another name beside his own. After a proper courtship, presided over and guided by Mordy himself, they were married in April in the parlor of Mordy's print shop. There was no honeymoon, because that very same day, before they had even consummated the marriage, Josef set sail to Florida to prepare their new home in the area he'd chosen from his guidebooks and maps because it was "beautiful and bounteous" and full of "hard-working men and women."

Josef and Lena both agreed that their life in Florida would forever be a honeymoon. Now Josef was wondering when that honeymoon would begin. Lena had been so frightened of the insects and small serpents that in nine nights together Josef and Lena had still not made love.

As the summer heat intensified, and the tropical nature of the land showed its lusty, primeval face, Josef knew that things were only going to get more trying for them both. He worried for Lena and for their marriage. He clung to what he could, to the ray of hope she'd given him this morning in coming out to the grove. But now this letter brought news that could threaten the bonds between them. Josef understood that Mordy had always been the cement in their relationship. He had introduced them, had encouraged their courtship, had planned the whole thing out for them—the hours they'd spend together, the chaperoned and unchaperoned outings, even the proper moment for a first kiss. It was almost as though they were characters in a romance of his uncle's making and for his uncle's pleasure. But even if they were, the very idea of pleasing his uncle had filled Josef with enormous warmth and gladness. Now his uncle was gone, and with him perhaps the best reason Josef had for feeling good about his marriage.

WHEN THE SMUDGEPOTS had all but hidden their house in an eerie gray smoke, Lena emerged from out of the trees and stepped up to the front porch, coughing at the fumes, but thankful for their effect on the mosquitoes. She had not been in the grove all morning as Josef had hoped. Shortly after Josef left, she'd thrown down her hoe in disgust at the heat and the bugs and the sweat that broke on her dainty brow and had run out to the ocean, crying, to wash her hands in the surf. There she'd sat all morning on a patch of grass under the shade of a palm, where she was still uncomfortably hot, but where the ocean breeze at least kept the bugs off her skin. She returned now because she'd been frightened away by what appeared to be an Indian woman approaching her up the beach. Of course, she wasn't going to tell any of this to Josef.

She found him with the letter in his hand and his head hung in sadness, and she knew exactly what the problem was. "Uncle Mordy," she said, knowing that he'd taken ill before she'd left Brooklyn, but until now keeping it from her husband.

"Yes," said Josef. "It's so. The man who raised me as a son, who taught me how to stand on my own and be an American. He is no more."

Josef broke down and buried his face in his wife's chest. She held him until he breathed a little easier. Then, with his hands resting on her thin hips, he looked up into her eyes.

"But there is something else that troubles me," he said. "Shoes. Mordy sent me leather shoes for my birthday."

"That was weeks ago, Josef," she said, waving the smoke from her face. "Why haven't I seen you wear them?"

"That's just it, dear Lena. I don't have them. They've never arrived, and now I fear they never will."

"Oh, don't say so, Josef," said Lena.

Just then it occurred to Josef what he'd read before he'd left Brooklyn about the mail delivery in South Florida. Because the deliveries from the North were often erratic and far between, weeks of mail might be delivered all at once. And thus, it was likely that the package from Mordy and the news of his death were scheduled to arrive at the same time. He marveled at how, this far from home, time could fall together like that, so that a celebration and a mourning would occur here all at once, while back in Brooklyn they'd been separated by weeks. But Josef felt cheated, having received only the latter. The gift of those shoes would have made him cry with joy at the same time he cried with sadness, because whether they'd been intended as such or not, in the special time of this exotic land the shoes were now a beautiful and painful final gesture from his adopted father and a powerful symbol of the bond and the love between them. Now all he had was Mordy's death and the horrible knowledge of this final gesture, forever incomplete unless the shoes found their way to the little post office across the lake.

He stood up, echoes of these thoughts thumping in his chest. Lena rubbed his shoulders, smoothed down the straps of his suspenders. She could not fully read his pain because of the smoke from the smudgepots, which drifted over and between them in waves, hiding and changing their features like magician's dust. At one moment Lena thought her husband looked angry and wicked, the next, brooding and insane, but she knew this was her own mind seeing in him what she saw as the true nature of the land to which he'd brought her. And when she chastised herself for seeing him in this light, she looked closer and saw that maybe he was just broken and frightened and in need of her comfort. Then, just for a moment, she forgot all her fears about their new life together and the doubts about her ability to stick by him as she'd promised so many times. In the closeness and comfort of the smoke she felt love, the way she'd felt it before they were married, when nothing else mattered but that they were happy and together.

"Listen, Josef," she said, speaking softly and reassuringly. "You will go to the post office tomorrow and inquire about the missing loafers. I think they will be found, and then things will be better. We'll have something to remind us of Mordy, and that will make us stronger."

Josef looked at her deeply, unsure of her expression but confident of the strength behind her words. He took her hand and kissed it.

"I shall," he said, repeating the words of his marriage vow.

The smoke wrapped around them like a pair of strong arms, and Josef prayed the feeling was no illusion.

Chapter 3

A STRANGE LITTLE FELLA with an accent," is how Earl described the new resident to Mely. He didn't know where the man had settled or if he had brought anyone with him. There'd been rumors that a man had been seen across the lake tending to a grove and building a house, but no one had bothered enough to go find out for sure. In the years since Earl's last publicity efforts, settlers had occasionally straggled into and out of the area; there was no reason to get excited about one in particular. If he remained more than six months, well maybe then it might be worthwhile to talk to him. Such was the attitude of the townsfolk. But for Earl, a new face always meant new possibilities, a chance, however small, of something exciting coming to pass. That small wistful pebble would glow briefly with hope, a ruby catching the light, even though nothing had ever come of new blood before. The settlers would always either move away out of fear or boredom, or assimilate into the cowardly, narrow mindset of the town. None of them ever shared Earl's bent for progress and success, not even in its diminished condition.

For some reason, though, Earl was enthusiastic about this new man. He already remembered the moment in the post office as something significant. He'd looked up from his mail sorting and his pool of regret and saw a picture of startling and dramatic beauty. He couldn't make out the man's face because of the glare in the doorway. But he knew that no one he'd met in Figulus had the dramatic awareness or even the dumb luck to make himself part of such a beautiful sight. And then, when the man approached the counter, Earl took in his unusual appearance (unusual for these parts, anyway)—his curly hair and dark, smooth complexion; his painfully erect posture and inscrutable eyes (was that wide-eyed innocence, disaffected irony, or merely a dull-minded glaze?)—and knew that he'd happened onto something remarkable. A man like this had to mean something, and Earl smiled in much the same way he'd smiled at the couple in the rocking chair when he'd first arrived in town.

So when the man had pulled the envelope from Earl's hand, Earl already had a feeling that the gesture was of great importance somehow and would one day warrant at least a comment in an autobiography of Earl Shank.

Then, just as suddenly as he'd come in and before another word could be spoken, the man gave Earl a nod of the head—the vestige, Earl figured, of some grand and exotic European greeting—and disappeared into the morning sunlight.

There were a million things he would have liked to have said, beginning with the basics, but of course guiding their words around to something more significant:

Gonna be another hot one. . . . Yep, summer's here to stay, I reckon. . . . Any breeze over yer place? . . . Oh, didn't know anybody'uz livin over there these days. . . . Bring yer wife down with ya? . . . Any little ones? . . . That's all right, you'll make some soon enough. . . . Yer young, with plenty a time. . . . Who me? Naw, always been too busy, ah guess—the mail never stops flowin, ya know. Like a mighty river, I reckon. And then there's always publicity work ta be done. . . . So there's that, too—that publicity. . . . Yessir, well . . . But say, what y'all growin over there?—Pardon? . . . Oh, you know, I do a little publicity work for the town now and then— attractin settlers, promotin commerce, that sorter thing.

Ain't a big deal. Keeps me busy, I reckon. . . . Oh, why sure,
sure. I kin always use a little help when things get too busy.
Course, it'd help most of all if ya happened to know a few in-
fluential folks up north. . . . Ya don't say? Well, then . . .

It might not have happened like that, but the results would
have been the same, because this was a man who got letters
from New York, a man with clean, pressed suspenders and
smooth, pink palms, and a man like that would have to know
people, a man like that would have to have friends.

Yet he'd let him go. He hadn't said any of the million things
he could have. He'd balked at a beautiful opportunity. Maybe
he'd grown rusty, or maybe he was finally beginning to slip
and take that long fall into old age and obsolescence. Or
maybe he'd gotten so used to failing and trying to forget the
failures that he'd grown afraid of success. But then a far more
reasonable explanation occurred to him: perhaps he'd happened upon something of such magnitude, such unfath-
omable importance, that that small, wistful pebble—or his in-
stincts, or whatever it is in a man's brain that makes him
recognize his destiny and reel it in—had told him not to rush
into it, had told him, "Whoah, Earl, this is the big one, let's
just slow down and play this thing right."

If the young man was a Yankee, he wasn't the first to settle
here—there were several long-time Yankee residents, though
they tried their best to make people forget that fact. And if he
was an immigrant, he wouldn't be the first of these either—in
the early days of the town, a pair of Finnish brothers had settled here, until they heard about a pair of Finnish sisters living
in St. Augustine. So there was no explaining it, not completely. The little man had done nothing more yesterday
morning than pick up his mail and leave. You couldn't even
say they'd had a chat. Earl hadn't even introduced himself,
fool that he was. There was something, though, in the man's
eyes and his perfect posture and the deliberate way he walked
that told Earl, *Now here's a young fella who might just stir*
things up. Though they looked nothing alike and probably had

little in common, the immigrant couldn't help but remind Earl of himself as a young man—determined, forward-looking, courageous and foolish at the same time. Still, even this didn't explain completely what he'd sensed in those moments; if he were later asked to write his memoirs, he'd finally have to give in to the dramatic and the serendipitous, knowing full well the outrage of the critics, and call it by name: destiny.

"A strange little fella with an accent," said Earl.

"I know what you're thinking, Earl," said Mely. She'd caught him before he slipped away this morning. "You leave that poor man alone," she said. "A new settler's got enough to worry about without you filling his head with your loony ideas."

"I just want to make the man feel welcome. Besides, hon, you know I've given up the loony ideas. I just got you, now." Earl grinned.

Mely tried to ignore him. "There's a leak in the roof needs fixin today," she said.

"Have to wait for the afternoon. Mail's in and there'll be people comin around all morning to check their boxes, you know."

"Seems to me the government could find a lot better things to do with their money than pay a man to sit all day on a stool and brush the mosquitoes off his face."

"Maybe so," said Earl, "but to me it's a kind and gen'rous government that provides us so."

With that, Earl was off to the post office before Mely had a chance to make him feel guilty again.

IT WAS ONLY EIGHT A.M. when Earl arrived at the office, but Josef Steinmetz was already there waiting for him. Josef had risen before dawn, having lain awake most of the night trying to think of a way to secure the missing loafers. As with all obstacles facing Josef, it was only a matter of methodically and logically thinking the problem through. Here was a problem: a misplaced pair of loafers. The proper solution had to be a sim-

34

ple, stepwise procedure. He had only to determine which tasks must be performed and then—the hardest part—order the tasks correctly to ensure success. Usually, thought Josef, when people fail it is because they don't think things through in an orderly fashion, and thus don't arrange the steps in the one proper building-block technique that will get the job done. Thus, Josef worried throughout the night exactly what he'd say to the postmaster and when, and what actions would be performed and when. The timing was so important.

Then, before Lena had so much as stirred, Josef crawled out from under their mosquito netting, dressed himself carefully so as to make a strong impression on the postmaster, and as the sun began its rise over the Atlantic, rowed his canoe the half mile across the lake to the little dock that marked the town of Figulus. Josef tied up his boat and stood outside the post office even though there was no lock on the door, because he thought it irreverent to wait inside a government building when there was no official on duty.

He waited two hours, sweating in the sunlight and afraid to move into the shade because the postmaster might show up at the wrong time and think he was loitering. Finally, Earl arrived and greeted him with a firm handshake.

"Pleasure to see you again, Mr. Steinmetz," he said, and he showed him into the office. Earl wasn't the slightest bit surprised that the man had returned the very next day; it only confirmed his belief in the significance of that first meeting. *Wouldn't it be a funny thing*, he thought, *if after all these years of pain and struggle, things'd finally fall into place on their own?* It occurred to him that such an easy success might well make a mockery of his earlier efforts, but he decided right then he could live with that.

Josef was silent and uncomfortable until Earl walked around behind the counter and they could address each other as postmaster and postal patron.

"What kin I do for ya?" asked Earl, resting his big hands on the counter.

"I am here to make inquiry concerning a missing postal item," said Josef, reciting exactly the line he'd rehearsed a hundred times on the canoe ride over and during his wait outside the door.

"Wellsir," said Earl, "what might that item be?"

Josef grew flustered already, not having written this part of the script. He'd been so concerned about making the proper impression himself that he hadn't anticipated the postmaster's responses to his inquiries; already, there was a hole in his plan. He was angry with himself and paused, stone-faced, while he decided what to do next. He debated whether he should reveal the exact nature of his package. Though he had great trust in his fellow man, he didn't think it wise to tempt the postmaster with a full description of the fine leather loafers a person can buy in the shopping district of Brooklyn.

"This would be a package," began Josef, now with diminished self-confidence marked by a slight hesitation and an even greater formality in his tone, "this would be a package containing a pair of shoes, addressed to myself, Josef Steinmetz, and originating from the city of Brooklyn."

Earl thought for a moment, stroking his chin. He wasn't thinking about the package, because he knew right away he hadn't seen anything that big come through. He was thinking that right at this moment he felt more like a postmaster than ever before. Or, more accurately, he felt more like a man playing the role of postmaster than ever before. The formality of this young man was like a gift of respect, far beyond what he received from his other postal customers. It made the whole transaction seem theatrical, and this brought Earl back all at once to his youth on the stage, a memory that previously had brought only the pain of his first failures. But now the fourth wall of the post office seemed to magically fall away and reveal a thousand pairs of eyes captivated by his remarkable and realistic performance as The Postmaster. It was a brief taste of the stage success he'd been denied in his youth. How sweet it felt to twist a past failure into something so satisfying. He was thankful for it, and for Josef Steinmetz, the supporting actor who'd made it possible.

"Nosir," said Earl, with a confidence that shone in the strength and depth of his drawl, a drawl straight from his diaphragm, "I ain't seen such a package come through here."

Josef stared at him like he'd forgotten a line, and Earl thrilled with the nervous energy this gave to the scene.

"No way of telling where that package is," laughed Earl. "Them folks in New York are liable to've shipped it off to Persia for all we know, and it's a funny thing to me that they don't more often."

"What about the carrier," said Josef, his plan collapsing in on him, his voice on the verge of cracking. "Can you not ask him?"

"Well, he don't like folks all that much, I guess. He drops the mail off after midnight, in the back there, and then he skips out of town 'fore anyone kin talk to him. T'tell the truth, I ain't never seen 'im," and he held up his hand like he was taking an oath to that effect. "Nosir, I reckon that's a dead end, there."

Josef looked down at his feet, at the pair of shoes he'd worn for three years. How pathetic they looked now when he compared them with the image of his uncle's gift. He felt defeated and embarrassed and could think of nothing more to say, so he went to the door slowly, head hanging, his brow breaking into a sweat.

Yet something made him stop. His best laid plans had crumbled before his eyes, but he owed it to Uncle Mordy, if not to himself, to take some sort of action. And then there was Lena to think about. Only yesterday, she'd begun to make progress in adjusting to their new home. She'd worked in the grove! That thought alone filled his heart and restored a little of his confidence. But he knew her faith in him had been shaken by her experience here. How could he face her after this? If he couldn't even get the postmaster to locate a missing package for him, how was he to tame the subtropical wilderness into a livelihood for himself and his wife?

He stopped in the light of the doorway. Then, looking up at the postmaster, approached the table again.

"Can I not leave a note for this carrier, perhaps on the back wall, where, as you have stated, he drops the mail?"

"It'll be dark out there," said Earl, now submitting himself to the natural flow of the scene. "And I ain't even sure the fella can read."

Josef thought some more, determined to maintain eye contact. "If I were to supply you with candles," he said, "perhaps you could . . ."

Earl admired the man's determination. He was reminded again of his younger self, which saddened and exhilarated him all at once. *This here's a man who gets things done,* he thought. *Maybe when I was younger if I'd just stuck with it . . . But maybe that don't matter now, maybe I kin ferget about that.*

The importance of the moment made him pause. What if he were to make the wrong move and destroy everything before it had even begun? *It would be just like me,* he thought.

"Hell, don't pay no mind about the candles," he said, finally. "I'll jes set my oil lamp out there. Course, I still ain't sure he can read, but there's a risk in everything, way I see it."

Josef nodded, inwardly bursting with the satisfaction of a task fulfilled. Earl brought out a fountain pen and sheet of paper from under the counter, and Josef wrote slowly, choosing each word carefully, taking a full fifteen minutes to complete it. Earl could only watch with amazement and admire the man's penmanship.

Dear Postal Officer,
    My dear uncle, who raised me like his own son, has recently passed from this earth. But some weeks before his death, he sent me a pair of fine leather shoes in a box from Brooklyn. This package has never arrived. Please, could you

check if it has been misplaced or misdelivered. My uncle was not a rich man, this is the one treasure he could afford me, and it is more precious to me than a chest of rubies or a team of strong mules. To aid in your search, here is the address from whence the package came. If found, please deliver to this postal office.

Your Faithful Customer,

Josef Steinmetz

Josef unrolled a piece of scrap paper from his pocket and copied down his aunt's address. And then, with a nod, he passed the pen and paper back to the postmaster and exited out into the morning, leaving Earl in an odd state of anxiety and excitement. And, of course, with a rousing applause ringing in his ears.

Chapter 4

WHEN JOSEF RETURNED to his house, he was jubilant with good news. From what had seemed like certain defeat, he'd stolen a victory. He'd made a plan, and when his plan broke down, he was able to think on his feet and adapt. *Adaptability! That's what pioneer life is about*, he thought. His Uncle Mordy and Aunt Lois had certainly adapted to life in Brooklyn. And think of all those West-reaching pioneers, adapting themselves daily to the harshest imaginable environments as they marched across the continent. Compared with their accomplishments, Josef's victory was small indeed, but it was a start. *In no time at all*, he thought, *I'll fit in like a local.*

He burst through the door like a new father, only to find his wife covered in mosquito netting. She was sitting at their dining table eating soup, her head and shoulders draped in the netting she'd taken from their bed. It covered her soup bowl as well, so that she had created a small, bug-free dining room for herself. When she saw Josef, she dropped the spoon and flipped the netting back over her reddened face.

Josef felt a sharp pang of betrayal. He knew she hadn't been out to the groves yet today. She was retreating again. He saw another side to it, though, because he had to. *Two steps for-*

ward, one step back, he thought. *My bride must set her own pace.* He smiled at her.

"You, too, are learning to adapt," he said.

"Forgive me, Josef," she said. "But the bugs! They are little vampires! We never had such big bugs in Brooklyn, and I'm afraid I don't have much more blood to give them."

"But dearest," said Josef, "they only desire something sweet!" He laughed at her, and she tried to smile, though inwardly she was already dreaming of her boat ride back to Brooklyn.

"Think of it this way, Lena. The more bugs in here, the fewer will be in our orchard, and the better our trees will grow. I say, Come in here, bugs! Make your homes in my bed for all I care!" And with this his exuberant mood got the best of him, and he pushed open the door and yelled out at all the bugs that still dared to linger in the morning sunlight. "Step right in, my friends! My glorious little bugs! My grasshoppers, my katydids, my armored scales and citrus mites, my ants, thrips, and aphids, my woolly whiteflies and mealybugs! All my buzzing little friends without shelter! Come in here, I say, and nourish yourselves! Drink of my blood, eat of my flesh! You're welcome, one and all!"

Lena, who had cringed at the very mention of these bugs, now squealed in terror and yanked Josef's arm back from the door. She shut it tight and slammed down the latch.

"You mustn't do that, Josef," she said. "You mustn't! I have worked all the morning to rid this house of bugs. I have swatted them with the broom and batted them out of the air. I have brushed and inspected every inch of our bed. You mustn't let them in!"

"But dearest," he said, approaching her. "Our grove—"

"I don't care about the grove!" she shouted, backing away.

"You can't mean that, Lena. I know you don't. The grove is our future. Have you seen it today? I believe our trees grew three inches in a single day. Why, our grapefruit trees are nearly to my shoulders!"

41

He stepped toward her and she retreated again. When he persisted, she picked up the mosquito netting and held it between them.

"How long are we going to remain here, Josef? When those trees are fully grown, will we leave then?"

Josef laughed. "Dearest, you act as though you know nothing of horticulture, and yet I presented you with four books on our wedding day, each dealing with a particular aspect of citrus growing."

Josef continued to move toward her, and Lena continued to retreat, mosquito netting still raised at arm's length.

"I didn't read them, Josef. I tried to read one, but it was so horribly boring I fell asleep."

"Darling, you disappoint me." Josef was genuinely hurt. To him, those books were like fairy tales whose theme was the romance and partnership of their married life. He couldn't imagine how they might bore her. Still, he'd do anything to keep her happy, so he smiled to mask his hurt. "Perhaps it's difficult for you to see the beauty in those books. But that's okay. It is always better to learn from experience. I'll be your teacher. I'll show you all you need to know, and as our trees grow to maturity, so will our love."

Lena started to cry now. "But I don't want to go in the grove again, Josef. I never want to leave this house again unless it's to go home."

She does not understand how much she hurts me, thought Josef. He struggled to keep his composure. Part of him wanted to lash out at her, and part of him wanted to cry. Instead, he remembered his victory earlier this morning, and this restored his hope. She needed time, that's all. In time she could not fail to see the pleasures of adaptation. He'd think of a way to get her out of the house again, and then she'd see that their new world wasn't such a bad place after all. Yes, he'd let her wear the netting. She could make a dress of it if she wished! But soon that shell would peel away, and she'd emerge in all her glory as a strong-willed pioneer woman. She'd fit in just like he did.

"Okay, my love," said Josef, "you needn't come out of the house until you wish to. I won't pressure you."

Lena, too, had decided to give in a bit, having thought with some regret about the sound of her words.

"I will try," she said. "I don't wish to fail you."

Josef kissed her on the cheek. They embraced lovingly, with the mosquito netting pressed snugly between them.

For lunch, Lena served Josef some pumpkin soup. As she ladled it into his bowl, he noticed that she seemed more at peace with the bugs that swirled around her.

"Would you like to hear about my meeting with our postmaster?" he said.

"Of course, Josef," she said. "It was selfish of me not to ask you."

"The postmaster was hesitant to aid me at first," he said. "But I pressed the issue and he heard me out. I devised an ingenious plan to contact the mail carrier himself, as he is apparently a mysterious and reclusive fellow. We'll hear from him now, I'm sure of it."

"I'm proud of you, Josef," said Lena. And she was. The strength of his optimism and his innocence charmed her thoroughly and reminded her of how she'd felt for him back in Brooklyn. In the days leading up to their marriage she seemed to have felt love for him all the time; now, sadly, such feelings made themselves known only after she'd purged herself of the anger and fear and discomfort that overwhelmed her in her new home. She smiled, but gave a shudder that caused her to spill some of the soup.

In the days that followed, Josef remained unable to lure his wife into their budding citrus grove, so he decided to read to her from his horticulture books. In the afternoons, he'd come in from the grove and describe to her the progress of their plants and what he'd done to help them grow. Then he'd read

43

aloud passages from his books, the same books she'd found so boring. But Josef was patient with her and paused, perhaps more often than was necessary, to explain what he'd just read. He hoped that by hearing these books read by the voice of a loved one, Lena would begin to take an interest in their contents. He didn't know that the only thing keeping her awake was her annoyance at having everything explained as though she were a small and not very clever child.

The exception to their little routine came once a week when, shortly before daybreak, Josef would dress in his cleanest suspenders and paddle across Lake Worth to the Town of Figulus Post Office, where he'd wait for nearly two hours until the postmaster showed up.

"I am sorry to trouble you," he'd say to Earl, introducing himself each time as "the man with the missing loafers," though of course Earl remembered his face and his name, but was all too pleased to adopt Josef's formality for the sake of the performance. Josef even gave in once and provided the postmaster with a few details about the elegant and shiny leather and the fashionable style of the shoes. He really had only a vague idea what the shoes might look like, but a few typical details, he felt, would make the shoes seem more real to the postmaster and make the search for them seem that much more urgent.

Earl looked forward to these meetings with Josef for their theatrical quality. He felt as though he was slowly erasing his early failure on the stage. And if he could erase one failure, then why not all the rest? Perhaps he could finally start over and one by one erase all the great failures of his life. He had no idea how this might happen, but he knew that for the first time in years he felt a real sense of hope.

"I am still awaiting word of my misdelivered shoes," Josef would say, straight-faced and staring with his wide, dark eyes.

"Wellsir, that carrier shows when he shows, if you know what I mean," and Earl would laugh good-naturedly with his hands folded before his belly, reveling in the continuing saga of these missing shoes. "But that note's still hanging out back there, if you care to look."

"No thank you, sir. That won't be necessary." But Josef would leave the office and walk in the opposite direction so as to circle around behind the building and cast a sidelong glance at the increasingly weathered, curling scrap of paper that now seemed to make light of his solemn request.

And that, for the next six weeks, was the extent of their meetings. Even when the mail made its rare appearance there was no sign of Josef's package and no indication that the mail carrier had bothered to look at Josef's note.

But the longer this went on, the more interested Earl became in this small, stubborn immigrant, and he wanted to know what that man was doing across the lake, and why he was so interested in a pair of loafers, shoes that would certainly be of no use to him here in Florida, where there were no dance halls, no broad avenues full of glitzy, high-priced shops and their wealthy, fashion-conscious customers, no theaters or restaurants.

"But there is a restaurant," Mely reminded him. "Right on the other side of that wall there. 'Stead of asking me questions about him which I ain't got no grounds to answer, why don't you invite him—and his wife, if he's got one—over to dinner. That's what I'd do, if I wanted to get to know 'em, which I ain't sure I do."

"Yes," said Earl, leaning back in his chair. "Yes, that's a fine idea, hon." And then he dozed off, forgetting this plan entirely until Josef showed up again at the post office.

"I am the man with the missing loafers," said Josef.

"Wellsir," said Earl, "I guess he shows when he shows." He laughed and shrugged, and then put his hands in front of his belly when he suddenly remembered.

Josef had already begun his exit, as if on cue.

"Wait, er, Mr. Steinmetz," said Earl. Josef stopped at the door. "Now I tell you what. I feel real bad about yer shoes and all. . . ." He was ad-libbing, now, but this scene had repeated

45

itself for too long, just like the recurring scene of his personal failures, and he'd finally decided to take action, to take control of this drama, as if he'd just bought the rights to the script. "Well, as a representative of the U-nited States Postal Service, sir, I feel obliged to, ah, make amends for our error. So how 'bout you come to my restaurant for a specially prepared gourmet meal. And bring the missus, if there is one. Say, Tuesday night?"

"Yes," said Josef, shocked and pleased at this unexpected display of friendship. "Thank you."

Just like that, Earl knew he had wrangled in the horns of fortune. His destiny had made itself known to him, having circled him for weeks, knowing it would take him that long to recognize what it was. He knew now that this young man was the bearer of his fortune, and Earl had only to sign for the package and then have the courage to open it.

He smiled at these thoughts as he watched Josef exit off-stage into the bright morning.

Chapter 5

A S HE PADDLED BACK across Lake Worth, Josef now found himself in a quandary. That mail carrier had never responded to his note, and things did not look hopeful in that area. Now, in accepting the postmaster's offer of consolation, he might also be accepting defeat. Perhaps he'd been too quick to accept the offer; he'd been thrown off balance by the postmaster's big smile and his own need to fit in. He'd let the postmaster off the hook, and the man would no longer be inclined to make inquiries for him or conduct searches along the postal route. The search for the package would not be taken to its next logical step.

Although Josef didn't have his uncle's gift, until this time he at least had had hope that he'd one day receive it. He considered that the next best thing. But now he'd retreated; he'd traded in his hope for a free meal and would probably never feel that fine Old-World leather snuggled against his pioneer's feet. All he had left was the painful knowledge of the shoes' senseless disappearance, tied forever like a string reminder around the memory of his uncle. His horror was that one day he'd have only the string reminder, that without the object of the gift, his memory of his uncle would fade, and with it everything that that memory had stood for—courage and conviction, strength and perseverance, love and duty, the values of the Old World, carried across the ocean from his father to his uncle, and with his uncle's death, left in the safekeeping of Josef himself. Though he tried to suppress them, he had doubts about his ability to keep the torch lit.

But one good thing might come of this. Here was a way to coax his wife out of the house. When he told her there was a restaurant in town and that they'd been invited to dine on the house, she'd be carried back to her days in Brooklyn. Then she'd see that things were not so different here, after all, that slowly the wilderness would be tamed just as Brooklyn had been.

He found Lena sewing at the kitchen table. She smiled weakly, pleased to see Josef but knowing that his return home meant another afternoon of horticulture lessons. It was difficult for Josef to detect her smile, since it was veiled by mosquito netting, which she'd taken to wearing most of the day now. Josef had gradually stopped laughing about it, and then stopped commenting about it at all. He'd made up his mind to let her ease herself in to their new life at her own pace. But she seemed to have stopped making progress, and the mosquito netting that separated them seemed to grow thicker all the time. The only time it didn't separate them was in their bed. Yet even there things weren't as they should be. Lena was still too uncomfortable and frightened of all the tropical night sounds to desire his attentions. Josef worried more and more about this at night, so much so that it clouded his mind and he couldn't think of a way to speak to her about it. So they lay there each night in darkness and silence, and when Josef finally drifted off to sleep it was into a dream-image of his wife wrapping herself, mummy-like, in thicker and thicker layers of mosquito netting. She seemed to have traded in her wedding veil for another one, and it felt like a sign of his own inadequacy that he could not lift it off. Did he not have the strength? Would he be reduced to the weakness of lies as his father had?

"I have good news," said Josef, hoping this would reverse that regrettable trend in their relationship.

"What is it?" said Lena. "Have they found the shoes?"

"No, dearest, but I have other news, news that I hope will cheer you up. In consolation for the postal error, the postmaster has invited us to dine at his restaurant Tuesday night."

Lena's eyes lit up at the word *restaurant*. Josef saw this and knelt down beside her. He held her hand as though he were renewing his marriage proposal.

"Listen, Lena. We'll dress in our finest clothes, as if we were going out on the town in Brooklyn. I will paddle you across and lift you out of the boat. I will help you into your chair and order the wine for you. And we'll dine by candlelight to the music of the tropics. At evening's end, we'll paddle back in the moonlight and, who knows, Lena, perhaps our romance will not stop there."

Josef gave her an embarrassed smile and Lena jumped out of her seat and hugged Josef tightly through her netting.

"Oh, yes, Josef! It's all so romantic! I can't wait! Please tell me more! Is it a fancy restaurant, like the ones your uncle used to take us to in Brooklyn? Do I have appropriate clothing? Because perhaps I can make something between now and Tuesday if you can find me some fine material. Will there really be music? And dancing?"

Before Josef could answer, she pulled herself away and began to rummage through her small chest of clothes for an appropriate dress. Josef smiled, though he felt the first pangs of apprehension as he realized how much depended on this dinner. In the following days, Lena was full of questions, most of which Josef could not answer to her satisfaction. He'd never seen the restaurant, and feared it might not meet her big-city standards for elegance. Still, he hoped the quaint atmosphere and the interesting local delicacies would help make pioneer life more agreeable to her. And if it did, he thought that perhaps they'd make a weekly habit of it. Something for Lena to look forward to as she worked in the grove.

49

Still, all of his hopes were tarnished by the loss of the shoes. He'd tell Lena, and wanted to believe himself, that perhaps it was Uncle Mordy himself who had intercepted the shoes, retrieving them for his long journey into heaven. "I like to imagine, Lena," he'd say, "that he has kept the shoes himself, and that at this very moment he walks in them as he walks with God." But even the beauty of this image could not erase the nagging feeling that he'd sold his uncle's memory for one short evening of comfort, that his plan had failed miserably.

As Tuesday approached, Earl worked hard to fix up the restaurant. It had deteriorated through its recent neglect, and now he suddenly felt the urge to patch up the roof, to steady some of the rickety tables and chairs, and to give the place a thorough cleaning, which made homeless a number of large insects and small nappy rodents.

Mely was amazed at his dedication to the task and wondered aloud why he wasn't so energetic about the household chores. But Earl didn't hear her; he was too busy. To him, this wasn't work. At least it didn't feel like work. Because now his mind, so long idle from the ravages of failure, had once again lit up in wild speculation. Earl was merely setting up the stage for his grand performance. He was his own stagehand, which suited him just fine, since that was the only way he could be sure things were done right. There was a lot riding on this performance, he thought, and he was a little worried about it. He knew that Josef and his wife were city folks, and Earl himself had never been to a big-city restaurant. Yet he wanted them to feel completely at home. If he could make a good impression on them, word about the restaurant might finally get out. Steinmetz would write home about Earl and his restaurant, and pretty soon people from up and down the East Coast would make a special stop—on their way to Biscayne or Key West or the islands—to sample the local delicacies at World Famous Earl Shank's. Of course, in no time at all he'd have to expand. He could borrow money for that, maybe hire a few of the locals. He could even sell shares and incorporate the restaurant. Probably shouldn't get too fancy, though; it's a good idea to keep some of that down-home country flavor. He'd become the paragon of Southern Hospitality. He'd be spoken of highly in places like New York, Boston, Washington. Admired for his shrewd business sense and his casual, almost effortless way of achieving success, as if he were one of those men walking in the golden footsteps of fortune, a man who couldn't fail. Then, at last, his previous failures would be erased; even if they ever came to light, no one would believe them, and he could feel safe in omitting them from his autobiography. Eventually, important people would come to see what all the hubbub was about. Candidates would come to court his influence on the state's electorate, and they'd bring all kinds of reporters with them, and one day one of them would turn to another and ask, "Well, why don't Earl Shank run for governor," and Earl could only smile—

"Earl, are you daydreaming again?" said Mely. "I thought you'd broke that habit." His wife, having finished her chores, had wandered next door to the restaurant, wondering at the silence. There she found Earl, standing in the midst of the small, dark dining room, grinning foolishly, his eyes glazed in thought.

"Well hon," he said. "I just got to thinking. If everything goes good with these Yankee folks Tuesdy night—"

"Stop what you're saying, Earl. I do not want to hear it. Understand me? Now I'll cook for 'em, best I can, but I know the kind of daydreams can float around in that big head a yours, and I do not want the future of the known world restin' on my shoulders."

"Yes, Mely."

Despite her chidings, Mely was strangely affected by what she called Earl's "daydreams." It had been a long time since she'd seen Earl so full of fanciful energy. He seemed younger than he had in years, and she remembered how Earl's big plans used to secretly excite her when they first got married. When he spoke of them he'd always seemed to her like a boyish adventurer, a swashbuckling romantic. Of course, this feeling faded when her husband's big plans fizzled under the constraints of reality. If he told her now the details of his plans, she'd only shake her head at his sad foolishness. But without the concreteness of the details, there was nothing to scoff at; there was only the dreamy youthfulness of reverie, which rekindled the excitement of years past. And with it, her desire.

She put her thick fingers on Earl's shoulders and kneaded them gently.

"There'll be plenty of time for fussin tomorrow, Earl. It's nearly dusk."

"Yes, Mely, I reckon you're right."

"Now why don't we hit the hay? We both need to rest up for our visitors."

Earl smiled and slipped his oversized arms around Mely's thick waist.

"I feel sort of girlish tonight, Earl. Like anything could happen."

"Might could," said Earl. "Might could."

They went to bed, and Earl figured that things were really looking up.

Chapter 6

On Tuesday, Josef and Lena dressed for dinner. Lena had begun early in the day, ignoring the mosquitoes for once to braid her long black hair and apply makeup to her smooth white skin. She picked out a silk dress of deep grays and blues, with gossamer ruffles at the neck and sleeves. She had last worn it in Brooklyn, on a night when Mordy and Lois took them out to see the variety shows.

Josef slicked his hair back, as he used to do in Brooklyn. He slipped into his only suit, the same one he'd worn to his wedding. When he slipped into his shoes, he hesitated a moment and thought of his uncle. How he wished Mordy and Lois were taking them out to dinner like old times! Only now, he thought, he and his bride might be moved into their own house back in Brooklyn, and his aunt and uncle would come calling to treat them to an evening on the town.

If only things had worked out like that! They could already have settled into a small, comfortable life. Josef would have ended his apprenticeship with Mordy and become a full partner in the printing business. Lena would be happily learning the skills of housekeeping instead of falling asleep during her horticulture lessons. She'd make some mistakes as she learned—burning the roast now and then or damaging some of Josef's clothes when she washed them. But Josef would only smile and his heart would fill at the earnestness of her efforts to please him. "Don't fret, dearest," he'd tell her. "Soon the printing business will grow and you'll have a cook and a housekeeper, and my beautiful young wife will join all the most fashionable ladies who stroll on the boulevard in their wide dresses and white gloves." In the meantime, Lois would come over and teach Lena the finer points of housekeeping, Old-World style, and while Josef worked all day in the print shop, the two women would talk about the best ways to keep him happy. "Our Josef likes his house clean and his bacon crisp." And soon enough, the house would be running smoothly and then they could make room for children. His heart would swell with the bliss of a household full of young ones. Josef imagined himself in a permanent state of joy and rapture. And all under the protecting arms of his dear Uncle Mordy, who'd one day pat him on the back and squeeze his shoulder, "Young Josef, I believe the time has come for me to retire," and the key to the print shop would fall neatly into Josef's breast pocket.

Oh, the warmth and sweetness of that life! He'd fought against his desire for it for so long and had tried to replace it with a life of his own making: Josef Steinmetz, the pioneer. He'd shunned comfort for something nobler—to create a new way of life from the ground up, a life from which others could benefit for generations to come. As a pioneer, he'd tame the malevolence of nature, while at the same time nurturing her good, until she was finally recreated in the image of man, and thus in the image of God. What could be nobler and more self-less than that? Yet more and more, he doubted whether he was up to the task, and these warm, sweet images of comfort began to torment him with their cruel and powerful temptations.

Far worse was when he let himself be carried away by such imaginings so that he'd try to make them concrete. He'd con-struct a detailed plan by which he and Lena could abandon Florida and return to Brooklyn to assume the sweet, banal life he believed was still there waiting for him. "We've had our youthful adventure, dear Lena, and now it's time to live up to our obligations. It's time to go home." But always there was something missing that prevented him from speaking those words: Mordy. When he walked himself through his plan, it would always end in some empty nightmare, alone in a room and with a hollow sound crying in his ear—the wind pressing at the door, or the creak of a floorboard in an empty room, or the echo of a leaky pipe—a horrible sound he was powerless to stop, a crushing, empty melancholy. He knew that with the death of Mordy, the bonds between him and his aunt and his young wife and all their children yet to come had slackened and fallen to the ground, and no one had yet come forward who was strong enough to pick them up again.

Because of that, Josef understood that he'd condemned himself to remain in Florida, for it really was the only way to test his strength, to determine whether he was worthy of pulling everything together again, the way it was in Brooklyn, and before. Mordy's death had locked Josef into an unspoken promise. He had to make a success of the life he'd chosen. To return now would be a failure and a disgrace to the memory of his uncle, one that would taint any comfort he might find back in Brooklyn.

Just as soon as Josef realized this, that sweet image of conjugal comfort redoubled the strength of its attraction and tore at Josef's heart with the rage of a shunned lover.

Tonight he put on his old shoes and hoped with all his strength that Mordy was looking down on him and Lena approvingly and would give Lena the strength to adapt to her new situation, and Josef the strength to fight off the horrifying image of a life he could never have.

EARL WAS WAITING outside the door when Josef and Lena walked up from the dock. He saw them coming down the path and straightened his best white shirt and the black trousers that he hadn't worn since his wedding to Mely, and which were too tight for him now. If he didn't keep them pulled up,

55

an unsightly roll of belly fat would hang over his belt. He'd have to watch for that.

He'd spent all day tidying up the restaurant, though it had been as clean and neat as it was going to get two days before. As a special touch, he'd planted torches on either side of the entrance. He stood beside one of them, ready to show in his guests.

"Pleasure to have you," he said, shaking Josef's hand. He turned to Lena. "This must be the little lady." He kissed her hand and Lena smiled, inwardly recoiling at his gross appearance and the coarse feel of his chapped lips on the back of her hand.

Josef knew right then that things weren't going to be all that Lena expected. Still, he put his hands behind his back and tried to maintain an air of refinement, despite the inadequacy of the surroundings. He said, ceremonially, "We thank you, postmaster, for your kind invitation. We are certain to dine on the finest foods the region has to offer."

"I reckon my wife's the finest cook south of Atlanta," said Earl. "And I ain't the only one who says it."

He led them inside and to a corner table by the only window. A candle had already been lit and placed on the patched-together piece of tablecloth.

There were eight tables in the place, yet Josef and Lena were the only guests. They settled themselves into the home-made chairs and looked around the dark room. There was nothing on the walls or any of the other tables. The window, glazed by the salty air, looked out on an impenetrable forest of cabbage palms and palmetto shrubs, which blocked out the few remaining minutes of twilight. The tree frogs had begun to chatter.

Josef looked at his wife, who couldn't quite muster a complete smile for him. Already he knew the evening was doomed.

When they were seated, Earl excused himself and disappeared out the back door, which was the quickest route to the kitchen next door. He was going to check how Mely was com-

56

ing along. But his mind had drifted to a time in the near future when his place would be full of rich Yankees, and he'd be passing from table to table hearing them talk:

"Oh, we must tell the Vanderbilts!"

"I've been thinking about building a railway line down here from Savannah, and now I—"

"You think this fellow Shank would like a few investors?"

"I think I could make it worth his while."

"The man's a financial genius, I say. Imagine parlaying a postal error into a thriving restaurant!"

"A gold mine!"

"Handsome devil, too!"

IN HIS RENEWED preoccupation with the restaurant, Earl had neglected his post office duties all week. He hadn't stepped foot in the place since the day he invited Josef for dinner. In the meantime, townspeople had come to drop off outgoing mail, and the outgoing mailbox was stuffed with a dozen letters and small packages. Earl hadn't been there to collect postage when they were dropped off, and he hadn't been there to catch up by registering the postage in his accounts receivable ledger. So of course he hadn't placed the outgoing mail in the mail sack and hung it on the nail in back of the post office.

Normally, this was of no concern to his mail carrier. It had happened before, owing to the carrier's erratic service and Earl's inability to predict when he'd show up. The carrier would simply drop off the mail he had and head south, thankful for the lightness of his load. But it had never happened on the first day of the month, and this concerned the mail carrier greatly. Because at the beginning of the month the carrier received his salary, a cash sum tucked into an envelope addressed to Andrew Jackson—another detail he'd worked out when he took the job. He received thirty dollars total, fifteen from the postmaster in Biscayne and fifteen from the postmaster in Figulus. This money was paid directly out of the postmasters' revenues, and he was now due his cash from postmaster Earl Shank, this being the first day of the month of September.

So this night, when he'd shown up early, anxious to get the cash so he could trade it for a pint of whiskey and make a night of it, he was greatly disturbed when he slinked around the back of the post office and found only a pair of rusty nails. He hadn't imagined that such a thing could occur. He'd imagined ripping open that envelope and the feel of the cash in his hand, and he'd imagined a speedy boat ride across Lake Worth and a brisk walk about twelve miles south, where he'd meet a middle-aged Indian woman on the shore of a little inlet as he did every month, and that Indian, in exchange for those fifteen dollars the carrier had no use for, would hand him a bottle of whiskey, one that had no label, yet was surprisingly smooth, as if the Indian herself were a connoisseur, had purchased it by the barrel and had blessed the carrier by parting with a precious portion of it. He'd imagined nursing that bottle as he leaned against a palm tree on the upslope of the beach, lulled by the sound of the waves and mesmerized by the brilliant night sky, until the potion took effect and for the first time in a month he ceased to feel the throbbing, grinding pain in his feet, and instead felt a peacefulness and a bliss that few men ever know as he mumbled aloud and sang himself to sleep.

That moment of paradise denied, he could not have been more angry. He squeezed his empty fists until his overgrown fingernails drew blood from his palms. Then, overcoming his reclusive bent, he stormed along the path at lake's edge, not knowing what this postmaster looked like, but in any case seeking someone to blame, until he stumbled and hobbled up to the first building he came to and pushed open the door to Earl Shank's restaurant.

JOSEF AND LENA were sniffing their wine when the man entered the room. They were trying to overcome the pungent smell and put the glasses to their lips, but now a new smell overpowered the wine. It was the smell of salty sweat and dried seaweed and clothes unwashed for months. The man was dirty and unshaven and carried a sack over one shoulder— he hadn't bothered to drop off the incoming mail.

Lena gave Josef a frightened look and he whispered for her to look away. He could think of no words to comfort her, and his brow beaded with sweat from the heat and from his growing anxiety.

The postal carrier looked around the room and realized he was in some sort of restaurant. He decided he'd demand to be served in exchange for his troubles, and then would threaten the proprietor, whoever that might be, unless his fifteen dollars was coughed up on the spot. He lurched his way over to a table and slammed his canvas bag on it, spilling the contents, acknowledging Josef and Lena with a sneer. Then he sat and waited for some table service.

As he did so, he began to shuffle through the letters and packages he'd spilled on the table. He grabbed a few of the letters, slit them open with his dirty and sunburnt finger, and began to read them, resting his thick hairy arms on the table, mumbling and grunting to himself and laughing scornfully at what he read of the intimate workings of families, friends, and lovers.

Josef worried about Lena. She was pale and trembling. He hadn't expected a fancy New York restaurant, but neither had he expected such filthy clientele. She stared out the window trying to collect herself, until a palmetto bug the size of her hand alighted on the glass. She shrieked loudly, pushing back her chair and covering her face. "Oh, Josef! Josef!" she cried.

Josef leapt up and flicked the glass for her until the monster disappeared. He patted his wife's shoulder. She took quick breaths, on the verge of tears. Josef felt suddenly like a trapped animal. That filthy man sat between them and the door. But even if they were to leave, then what? There were millions of bugs out there, all of them, as Lena said, like tiny vampires. There was a whole subtropical jungle of swarming, malevolent creatures. He knew it would drive Lena mad to go out there now in her condition. He and Lena were caged animals who understood that the safest thing was to stay in the cage.

The stranger across the room had turned in his chair when Lena shrieked. Now Josef became conscious of his stare. The stranger looked them up and down, taking in their dress, their neatly groomed appearance, the unshakable polish of citified Yankees. Then, with a sneer, he turned back to another letter he was in the process of opening and, shaking his head, grumbled, "Damn Yankee pigeons." Then, louder, "Yankee rats! Carpetbaggers!" He slammed his knuckles on the table, glowering.

Lena covered her face and began to cry now. Josef was still standing, wondering now what he ought to say to the unkempt stranger, wondering if this was grounds for something more serious than words.

The postmaster interrupted his thoughts, returning from the kitchen with their dinner. He stopped short when he saw the stranger, mystified and then pleased.

"Are you here to dine with us, sir?"

"Well, I sure as hell ain't here for the company."

Earl brought the platter to Josef and Lena's table. Lena made a half-hearted effort to pull herself together as Josef returned to his seat.

"Here you are," said Earl, lowering the tray to the table. "Fresh gatortail in wine sauce."

Lena took one look at the footlong hunk of steaming reptilian flesh, with its warty skin and dragon-like ridges, and ran from the restaurant holding her mouth.

Josef called after her, "Lena! Lena, come back!" He pushed aside the postmaster and made for the door, but he stopped short when he heard the stranger laughing mockingly. Josef felt it was his duty to say something. He had his wife's honor to uphold. If he was ever going to prove himself a man to her he ought to challenge this blackguard here and now. And he'd do it as they did in the Old World, with pistols and steps. He'd show this ruffian whom he was dealing with. He remembered

60

a story his Uncle Mordy had told him about a great grandfather of his who had once fought a duel and got his ear shot off. Josef could think of no better honor than to lose an ear for Lena.

With all the courage of his Old-World lineage behind him, then, Josef stepped up to the stranger's table and slapped his bristly face.

The man stopped laughing, startled. Earl remained in the shadows, hoping for one of those good old-fashioned barroom brawls that would win his restaurant great renown.

"Now that's a place with some real action!"

"Like the Wild West—only with a beach!"

"Sir," said Josef, "you have offended my wife with your impolite remarks and your brutish smell. I demand satisfaction for her honor."

The stranger rose, looked him in the eye, and drove his fist into Josef's face.

Chapter 7

JOSEF AWOKE IN the Shanks' kitchen, gasping in pain as Mrs. Shank tended to his broken nose. Morning light poured in through the open window.

"Keep still," said Mely, "or you'll start bleeding again."

Earl came into the room carrying another damp rag. He wasn't convinced that things had gone well last night. The Steinmetzes weren't going to write home about the food because they'd never tasted it. But there was that Wild West angle, which had a certain undeniable attraction. Most rich Yankees wanted some form of thrill these days, especially the idle rich, and why risk real danger when they could come to:

Earl Shank's
Wild West Steakhouse
Barroom Brawls and Shoot-'em-up Shows Nightly.

Of course, there were logistical headaches. He'd have to breed cattle, and for that he'd need to clear some grazing land.

He'd have to think about this. In the meantime, he'd have to play the whole event like it was natural and expected.

"Well, if it ain't Sleeping Beauty," he said.

"It ain't," said Mely. "Not with a nose like this."

Josef's nose was purple and swollen grotesquely, and his eyes drooped under the weight of the puffy black bags beneath them.

"You was out good, I'd say," said Earl. "You ought to see yerself. That feller gave you a fine pair a shiners and a crooked nose in the bargain. If I didn't know better, I'd think he mighta put you away for good, and now you're rose up just ta haunt us. Don't he look like a ghost, hon? You better check his pulse, jes ta be certain."

"Don't be ribbin the man when he's injured," said Mely.

Josef had slowly regained his faculties, and remembered the night before in brief, nightmarish flashes.

"Yessir, you'll be writin home about this, and 'fore you know it, all yer friends up in New York'll want ta come down for a souvenir like you got."

"Where's Lena?" said Josef.

"I expect she's back home, worried about you. She don't know you been decked."

Josef forced himself to his feet despite Mely's protests. He ran out the door, and Earl called after him, "Hey, Mr. Steinmetz! Funny thing about that feller who hit you! Turns out he was the mail carrier! Same feller who lost your package! Looks like he done you double dirty! He'uz just lookin for his salary, that's all, but I fed 'im yer gatortail an' he calmed down nicely! Said it was delicious! Hey, take my skiff there, by the dock! It's okay, you can take it! Come back and try that gatortail sometime, all right, Mr. Steinmetz?!!"

Josef paddled the postmaster's skiff across the lake, then ran along the edge of the grove to his home, where he expected to find Lena, worried half-sick about him, overjoyed that he was safe. She'd tend his wounds, and all would be forgiven.

Instead, he found a note:

Dearest Josef,

   I am not as brave as I once thought. This place frightens
me, like a storybook tale of the dark jungles of Africa. I can
no longer sleep for fear of the flying beasts, and this heat is
too much for my frail constitution. I am weak, Josef. I have
failed you.

   This morning, an Indian woman came to the door. She
frightened me at first, but she was refined for a savage and
spoke perfect English. I was desperate, Josef, and my desperation was stronger than my fear, so I asked the woman to take
me to Biscayne so I could catch a steamer back to Brooklyn. I
paid her our last twenty dollars. Can you ever forgive me?
No, don't try, I am not worth it. I am the worst wife a man
could have, I am a traitor to you.

   Don't follow me, Josef. I know how much this life means
to you. It is your dream, and the dream of your fathers. Do
not give it up on my account. I will always be yours in spirit,
and will remain true, despite my failure as a wife. Goodbye,
my love.

   Your Lena

Josef wept uncontrollably, slumped beside a chair in the
center of the small house he'd built for his marriage. He felt
the coldness and the emptiness of the room, empty of Lena's
clothes, Lena's perfumes, empty of Lena, eating her soup behind her veil of mosquito netting.

   He crumpled the note, then uncrumpled it, smoothing it
out on the chair and reading it again and again, hoping to find
a word or phrase he'd missed before, something to give him
hope, or something to tell him she'd only played him a cruel
joke, one he well deserved for his cowardly hesitation in de-
fending her honor.

   Then his grief turned to anger. What a foolish and stupid
idea to think he could bring his wife here to this hellish jungle
and expect her to be happy! How stupid to think himself as
brave and industrious as his forefathers, to think he could
conquer this wilderness with his two soft, small hands! He
was glad those loafers had never reached their destination; he

was not worthy to wear them, and he was not worthy of any gifts from a man as great as his uncle. It was God's will that they were lost. It was a sign, but he'd been too thickheaded to see it. He was weak and stubborn, and now, as punishment, the Lord had taken his wife from him. How stupid he'd been!

He kicked over the dining-table chair. Then his eye fell on the bottle of kerosene in the kitchen, and he grabbed it and ran out into his citrus grove. With tears streaming from his blackened eyes, he doused a dozen of his best trees, ones that were nearly ready to bear their first fruit.

This is what my dream amounts to, he thought. *This is how weak and stupid I am!*

He set the trees aflame. As if that weren't enough, when the fire took hold he shook the trees and kicked them, trying to break their trunks, burning his palms and tearing them on the splinters, until he could no longer breathe through the smoke, and he stumbled back to his house, collapsing on the front porch. A feverish mixture of sweat and tears stung his cheeks, and he watched his orchard burn in the bright, terrible sunlight.

WHEN HE FINALLY collected himself enough to think again it was nearly sunset, and the air had grown quiet in the brief lull between the last singing of birds and the first chirping of insects.

He walked out into his orchard. There was nothing now but rows and rows of black, leafless trees. Their last embers still hung in the air, winking out, and the ground was gray with ash. He reached just above his head and pulled from a smoldering limb what would have been the first fruit of his grove. It was small and immature, and he couldn't tell whether it would have been a grapefruit or an orange. Now it was coated with ash, and when he squeezed it in his fingers, it crumbled dryly to his feet.

There was nothing here for him now, and his first thought was that perhaps he should follow Lena. He worried about her when he recalled the Indian woman she'd mentioned in her note. Josef had not seen any Indians in the area, though since he had never seen one in his life, he wondered whether he'd know one if he saw one. Why would an Indian approach their house? What business would she have? But worse, it troubled him greatly that Lena would be in such a state of mind that she would travel alone with a savage. For all she knew, this squaw might take her directly to the big chief, who'd imprison or enslave her on the spot.

He shook his head, sadly. *Lena, Lena*, he thought, *how could you?* His impulse was to follow her down to Biscayne in the hope that she'd actually made it there. If so, he could surprise her on the steamer, beg her forgiveness, and then renew their marriage back in the city, where they belonged. Maybe it took something like this to make that comfortable little life possible again, he thought. The memory of these difficult days could only serve to draw them closer together. Nothing binds more tightly than a shared disaster. One day they'd gather their children together and tell them the whole tragicomic tale of their brief days as pioneers. It would be hard for the children ever to believe that their parents had been pioneers, but they'd retell the story anyway, simply because it made such a good story, and the story would perpetuate itself like that—a story told out of habit, for the sake of the telling, even though the teller did not fully believe his own words.

But this image of a family story was too like the memory he had of his family's dissolution and his father trying desperately and pathetically to keep them together by telling stories he did not believe. Now Josef had caught himself lying in the same way. He'd made a sweet illusion for himself, like the romantic convent on his family's wine labels. He saw his family gathered around the wine tubs the way they used to, making things pretty, telling themselves lies, blissful and smiling in their foolish ignorance. It had been only a matter of time until those beautiful lies showed their second faces and revealed themselves to Josef as nothing more than selling tools. They'd worked on Josef; he'd bought them, and used everything he had to do so. But he was not going to let it happen again.

He shuddered and cursed himself for his weaknesses. How could he think of returning? He'd never be able to face his Aunt Lois. He'd have disgraced the memory of his dear uncle, and he'd never be capable of respecting or redeeming himself again. Every time he read a news report about the growing opportunities in Florida (and there were sure to be many) he would cringe with shame, knowing that so many others were succeeding where he had failed. No degree of success in Brooklyn could ever erase the humiliation of his failure as a pioneer.

Come what may, he resolved, Lena would have to survive without him. It was she who'd left him, after all, and for what reason? A few words of impoliteness by a native who doesn't know any better? A few harmless insects? Her disdain for the local cuisine? Well, she could return to Brooklyn and face her shame. Perhaps it would even do Lena good to spend time in the Old Country, where everything was settled and safe, where the hard work had already been done. But Josef would stay here and brave it out as Mordy and Lois had when they first came to America. Aunt Lois would understand. Certainly she hadn't taken a steamer back to Austria the first time she'd encountered a rude, uncultured American. She and Mordy must have had their difficulties, but they'd stuck it out and made a place for themselves.

Out of respect for his uncle and also for himself, Josef reaffirmed his commitment to the pioneer life—wifeless now, if that was the way fate would have it.

The sky had turned thick and dark, and the insects began to circle Josef's head. He dragged himself into his house and, seeing the mosquito netting balled up on the dining-room table where Lena had left it, took it to bed with him and pulled it over him like a blanket. Though he'd gained strength in his new resolve, he still could not help but dream of

67

Lena and what might have been, what should have been, his fortune.

IN THE MORNING, Josef resigned himself to go across the lake and seek employment, perhaps as a mate on a fishing boat, or a field hand on one of the small farms, or, if he had to, as a waiter in the postmaster's restaurant. He'd replant his grove some day, but now he hadn't even the money for seeds. He thought it would be good for him to place himself in a position where he could interact with and learn the ways of the local population.

He shaved and washed his face, crying out in pain whenever he brushed his swollen nose or his blackened eyes. Then he wrote a note out to prospective employers:

To Whom It May Concern:
    I, Josef Steinmetz, attest that I am young, strong, honest, and industrious. I seek employment for fair wages wherever it is needed. I have numerous labor skills, and am knowledgeable in the science of horticulture. I hold no grudges against those in authority, and I do not get seasick on small boats. References available upon request.

He copied this résumé five times over, to post around town and to leave with men with whom he'd inquire personally.

He brought a hammer and tacks with him, too, and when he got off the boat in front of the post office, he nailed one résumé to a post on the dock.

When he entered the post office, he found the postmaster and his wife sorting mail behind the counter.

"Look, Mely," said Earl, falling immediately back into the role of sarcastic Wild-West bartender, "it's that ghost from across the lake."

"Don't make fun of the man, Earl," said Mely. "His nose is broken and he has you to thank."

Earl looked at her with annoyance. She had upstaged him already.

Josef was eager to get on with business. "I do thank you for your kindnesses," he said, and began the little speech he'd rehearsed on the way over. "I hope I do not impose myself on you at the present time when I present you with my résumé. I seek employment, and since you, postmaster, are familiar with all the townsfolk, I'm hoping that when they come to you for mail you will bring up my name within the context of honest men who seek steady employment, if such a context were to present itself in your conversation."

Earl took the résumé from him and looked it over.

"Wellsir," he said, "we'll see what we kin do. But first you'd best let Mely bandage up that nose of yours. People'll think you're looking for a job as town ghoul."

"Watch yerself, Earl," said Mely. She motioned for Josef to come behind the counter. He did so nervously, feeling like a spy or an intruder there on the government side of the counter.

Mely disappeared to go get some bandages. She was the closest thing the town had to a nurse, simply because she wasn't squeamish about it.

Josef was left in an uncomfortable position, alone with the postmaster and out of his usual role as customer. He couldn't think of anything to say.

Earl, too, felt somewhat uncomfortable. He'd played postmaster to Josef's postal patron, and he'd played maitre d' to Josef's restaurant guest, but now there was no script, there were no easy lines. It was an entirely new situation, and Earl felt a lot depended on it. He still had high hopes for the ultimate success of his restaurant, but he knew, after the incident a couple nights ago, that the chips could fall either way. Later, when he thought again about this moment and about how he'd nursed a new role out of seeming chaos—and what a role it turned out to be! a role with eminence and majesty, a role with more power and beauty than he'd ever thought imaginable!—he'd have to say that the role was written for him by fate itself.

When Josef had been knocked to the floor that night in the restaurant, Earl had confronted the offender, albeit meekly.

"There weren't no need for that," he'd said to him, not yet understanding that what had just happened could be turned to his advantage. "There just weren't no need for it."

Then the dirty man grabbed Earl by the shirt, got up in his face and demanded fifteen dollars for his services to the community.

And it hit Earl all at once who this man was and why he felt neglected. He apologized profusely, gave the man his wages, fed him the Steinmetzes' dinner, and sent him on his way. A cozy feeling came over him then, like he'd just uncovered some forbidden information that could help him in some yet undiscovered way.

Today he found a use for it.

Earl broke the silence. "Way I understood it, you was working on an orange grove across the lake."

"I've decided to hold off cultivating the land until I better acquaint myself with the local settlers and their customs," said Josef.

Earl felt a faint shudder of nerves. Many things were happening at once, and he wasn't sure what it all meant. This man had been tossed upon his shore like a formless and unknown sea creature. What did it mean? Was it a gift? It had to be a gift.

Earl tried to remain calm, sorting and re-sorting the mail, keeping his eyes on that until Mely returned with the bandages.

"Now, how 'bout that pretty little wife of yours," said Earl, "if you don't mind me askin. You going to leave her alone all day?"

"Earl," said Mely, admonishing.

"I have sent my wife back to Brooklyn," said Josef, now reciting the little speech he'd prepared to explain this fact. "She is unwell, and it's better for her to wait there until I have

70

established myself in this area. It was a mistake to bring her here so soon."

It wasn't really a lie, Josef told himself. Yesterday, he would have been ashamed to distort the facts this way. But now, as he spoke the words, he believed them fully.

"You tell them folks in Brooklyn to fatten her up some," said Mely. "A gal down here has to be strong."

"That's right," said Earl. "Down here there ain't no women's work and there ain't no men's work, there's just work and lots of it. Everybody's got to do his share. Least, that's what Mely says."

"Most folks do a fair share," said Mely. "But folks who're married to men with a government post seem to put in a little extra. I hope, for yer wife's sake, you stay away from a government post."

"I reckon a government man has to sacrifice certain pleasures in service to the nation." Earl was about to elaborate on this when he was struck dumb by a brilliant thought. Once again, he owed Mely a debt of gratitude for planting the seed. This young immigrant, this gift of fortune, had come to him this morning looking for a job, and now Earl had found one for him. It was true genius, because he needed to keep this man under observation. He needed this man to work for him.

"Listen, er, Mr. Steinmetz. I believe I have somethin you might be innarested in. I didn't mention it before 'cause I didn't want to embarrass you. But I felt so bad about that trash-talking feller dustin yer snout, I went and got him fired. Matter of fact, I just wrote out the letter to the Postmaster General before you came in this morning. It might take a few months traversin the proper channels, gettin approved here and there in all the high places. But it's within my authority, in emergency situations like the one facing us now—I mean, what bigger emergency could there be than a town without mail service—so it's in my authority to appoint an interim postal carrier until such time as the new hiring is approved, at which time I may just waive the probationary period, owing

71

to yer months of interim duty, and you will be promoted to official postal carrier for the U-nited States Government."

Mely gave him a stern look, knowing it was all a lie. But for Earl it was only a half-lie, or at least one he could make true.

Mely pressed bandages onto Josef's nose. He flinched in pain until he realized the great opportunity the postmaster was giving him. His eyes came alive.

"Do I stand a chance of qualifying?" he said. "That is to say, I feel confident I could meet the challenge of such a position, but surely I am up against experienced candidates."

"No," said Earl, shaking his head. "Lucky for you, you're the first man to apply. Now, as far as meetin the qualifications, well les jes see here." He picked up one of Josef's hand-written résumés.

"Careful now, Earl," said Mely, still affixing bandages to Josef's face.

"This is official government business, Mely," said Earl. "You don't understand about it."

"I never heard of the government conductin monkey business."

"Then you ain't never worked for the government, Mely."

Sure, it's a kind of game, he thought. But he knew it had far-reaching implications. This was more than play-acting. This was the key turn of events in the story of Earl Shank. The world would know that one day. The whole world would celebrate how his sense of humor did not fail him in a moment thick with majesty. He had the ultimate composure. And when the rest of the world was finally convinced, then maybe even Mely would regret her short-sightedness at the Primary Moment.

"Okay," he said, holding the note. "Yer young and strong— that's good, there'll be lots and lots of walkin to test them young legs. 'Honest,'—that's good too, because a carrier needs all the friends he kin get. 'Industriess'... well, you never know when that might come in handy. Oh, and horticulture—well that's a must-know in case you get stranded with no food nor water—you could just plant some seeds and wait for the fruit. I don' mean to scare you off with my talk, Mr. Steinmetz, but this ain't the easiest job."

Josef straightened himself. "I am prepared to endure great difficulties," he said.

Earl leaned back and gave Josef a final inspection, taking in those old shoes and the still-new suspenders and unsullied shirt, and read Josef's eyes for the first time—the earnestness and also the painful innocence. He wondered if he was doing the right thing in sending this man out onto the beach route. The young immigrant was hardly an ox—still somewhat soft and pale and citified, as a matter of fact. And he didn't strike Earl as a vessel of practical knowledge. It was obvious, though, that the man had a big heart, and whatever else made Earl waver in this decision was quickly overcome by that recognition. In this moment Earl forgot completely the pain of his past failures and recognized only the beauty that was about to emerge from all of them. The young man deserved a chance to fail as Earl had, but also to share in the glory of Earl's success.

"Wellsir, Mr. Steinmetz, I do believe you meet the qualifications. Given the urgency of the situation, I won't be required to check yer references. Welcome to the Government." He held out his thick hand.

Josef took it and gave him a firm shake, clenching his teeth against the pain from his burns and splinters.

"Show up tomorra morning ready for a long walk," said Earl.

Josef left.

"I'm surprised he didn't tell you and the U-nited States Post Office where to go, way you was treatin him," said Mely.

"Just havin a little fun, Mely."

"At another man's expense."

"What a fella don't know don't hurt 'im."

"Well, I don't reckon you know if that little man's goin ta hold up out on that beach. And I reckon not knowin that, and not knowin a single thing about this man, could get you a mighty big thrashin comin out of Washington."

"Well, I read his résumé, Mely. You heard me—he's strong, honest, and industriess, and what more could a body ask for? A man's got to trust in his fellow man. That's the way things work around here, you oughtta know that. And when in Rome, et cetera."

"Keep daydreamin, Earl. See if it don't land you out of a job."

Earl was thinking now about Josef, imagining that he had gone right home to write all his relatives and tell them about his new job and about the kind postmaster who'd hired him, and about the kind postmaster's remarkably quaint little restaurant in the middle of the Florida jungle and, though he didn't get to taste the food, he'd been able to smell it, and could attest to the delicate aroma of the fine cuisine that most certainly is served there, making the restaurant a must-see on any trip down the Florida coast, should any of his relatives or their friends be inclined toward a little tropical holiday.

"Earl," said Mely.

But Earl could not be shaken out of this daydream, for he knew that the young immigrant was the embodiment of his fortune. And now Earl was boss.

Chapter 8

A s Josef returned to his little house, he was deep in thought, not so deep that he'd forgotten that his wife had left him, but deep enough that he permitted himself to indulge in thinking about her and about the things he'd say to her if she were still at home and things were as they should be. He imagined how proud she'd be of him that he'd landed this job, how she'd look at him with new eyes, full of undying faith and confirmed love. She'd grow sorrowful as she helped him prepare for his morning's journey, but he'd tell her that it was only for a short time, and if they endured this one hardship their lives would change for the best, their marriage would strengthen, and they'd learn to love what they could not always have in front of them to hold and care for.

But just as soon as Josef stepped into the empty house, his little fantasy was shattered into the shards of vanity he knew it to be. His wife did not possess that kind of strength, and he had not possessed the faith to imbue her with it. He had to put that behind him now and hope that his new experiences would fill him with the perseverance he'd been waiting for. He was determined to make his Uncle Mordy smile down upon him.

"Show up ready for a long walk," the postmaster had said. If only he had those fine loafers to wear. Nothing would have made Mordy happier than for Josef to write him explaining how he'd begun a new job working for the United States Government and how he was going to perform his duties in the fine leather loafers he'd received for his birthday. But then, if it weren't for the missing loafers, Josef thought, none of this would have occurred, and he sensed for the first time that mysterious powers were at work shaping the events of his life in Florida.

He knew he had to do something to make his uncle proud, for those times when Mordy looked down from high above and could know that he was remembered by his survivors. He couldn't wear the loafers, but there had to be something else.

He slept little that night, turning over and over as his mind did the same to come up with a fitting act of devotion for the uncle who'd made all this possible.

WHEN JOSEF RETURNED to the post office early the next morning, Earl was waiting for him behind the counter.

"Glad to see you, Mr. Steinmetz. Lookee here." He pulled a sack from behind the counter and set it on top. "My wife's cooked you snapper, and thrown it in this sack with some fruit and vegetables. There's enough for a round trip, if it holds up in the sun. But anyway, that postmaster in Biscayne ought to give you something. I put a note in to him along with the rest of the mail, tellin him the situation, that that ornery SOB's been fired and from now to make sure that only *you* get the mail."

Then Earl pulled out an official postal sack, emblazoned in blue with the postal insignia, eagle and stars encircled by the words *United States Postal Service.* At the sight of it, Josef's heart swelled with pride. He was going to contribute to the very operation of this vast and wonderful country, his adopted home.

Earl embarked on a full description of the postal carrier's duties and routes, and what he might expect along the way. He gave him the pep talk about how Josef was now a link in the great chain of mail delivery stretching across this great, proud land. Josef listened earnestly. "And as you know," said the postmaster, "a chain is only as strong as its weakest link. Now down here in Florida, that chain is just as thin as a lone man walking the beach for sixty miles at a stretch, and I feel obliged to tell you that that lone, thin link yer about to walk is full of serious dangers, both natural and man-made, evil things that try their dangdest to stretch that link to its breakin point, thereby leavin the great chain of the United States Postal Service danglin free and easy in the wind, allowin any ol' body to come along and pull it at one end, thereby ringin the bell at the other. And sir, that bell is none other than your true boss, the President of the U-nited States —a man who does not appreciate gettin his bell rung."

Josef felt grave with responsibility. "Postmaster," he said, "I am ready to accept the duties of United States Postal Carrier, and I pledge to fulfill them to the best of my abilities."

Earl couldn't wait to get home and tell his wife about this, and then have her give him that look, chastising him, yes, but also, Earl knew, sharing at some level in the joke.

"You're all right, Mr. Steinmetz," he said. And he meant it. "I believe you'll make a fine carrier. I really do."

Then, finally, Earl pulled out one last item from behind the counter. "I almost forgot," he said. "The shoes."

These were the official Postal Service shoes, he told Josef. Designed by a team of government scientists for maximum comfort and durability. They had rubber soles and canvas tops and the postal insignia stamped on the side. One size fits all.

Josef had other ideas about this, though. "Postmaster," he said, "I have one condition to add to our verbal employment contract. I must be permitted to forgo the use of the Postal Service shoes, though I can see they are fine shoes, well-suited to my walking requirements."

"I don't understand. They're free."

Josef's face reddened. He hadn't anticipated any resistance to his idea. "I understand this, sir. But I've made the decision to perform my duties without shoes, in honor of my late Uncle Mordy and the fine loafers I never received."

Earl wasn't sure if Josef's words were a sign of hostility, perhaps a bitterness resulting from what Josef still perceived as Earl's failure to locate the shoes. He didn't want to press too hard and upset the man.

"Wellsir," he said, "I remain sorry about them shoes. But I wouldn't suggest you go barefoot out on that beach. Yer feet'll turn to soup 'fore you get halfway to Biscayne."

Still, Josef held firm, explaining that it was a risk he was willing to take, that if he received blisters on his feet, it could only add to the tribute he was paying to his Uncle Mordy, who'd raised him as a son, and whose gift of fine loafers seemed to have been lost forever somewhere between Brooklyn and Figulus.

So the postmaster could only shake his head, thinking, *This is one odd feller. He ain't gonna last two days, and then where will I be?* Earl hadn't figured that his fortune would have a mind of its own, would acquire a death wish so soon after revealing himself. Perhaps, he thought, fortune is like an excessively modest woman who would rather destroy her body than have it exposed to the world. Another question nagged him from the back reaches of his brain: that perhaps he'd been wrong about everything, that this man was nothing more than a foolish young immigrant who was going to kill himself through his own stubborn ignorance. But the events had been too neatly ordered for that, he knew. There must be some purpose to them all. In any case, there was little he could do now. The mail had to run; fate would have to take its course.

Josef loaded himself up with the postal sack, the small sack of Mely's cooking, and a canteen that the postmaster had filled with water for him. He shook hands with Earl one last time and walked proudly out into the early light.

Earl feared it would be the last he'd ever see of the strange foreigner. *That is one odd feller*, he thought, trying to laugh to

78

himself, but unable to cover up the feeling that he'd just sent a man to his doom.

That night, when he told his wife all this, about the pride he'd seen in Josef's eyes as he accepted the postal sack, and Josef's firm refusal to accept the postal shoes, and the pain he felt at watching Josef leave, she hugged him and cried at the most genuine display of feeling she'd ever seen in her husband. And when she did so, he suddenly saw it her way, and he had to admit his eyes got kind of cloudy too.

PART II

The New Paradise

Chapter 9

WHEN JOSEF EMERGED through a path in the sea grapes and took his first step in the sand, he became one of the few travelers on the great Florida highway—the wide, white, powdery beach linking Jacksonville with Biscayne and all points between. This was the route of the U.S. Postal Carrier—no company, no traffic, and long, empty miles between post offices. It was the kind of emptiness to give you the feeling that anything might happen at any time, though usually it did not.

The morning was blanketed by a ragged cloud cover and at first the sand felt cool and wet, like a sponge bath, on Josef's bare feet. He felt like a young boy again, curling the sand between his toes as he made tracks in the smooth, white surface. He couldn't help but think again of those first years in America, when Uncle Mordy had taught him to swim in the Hudson River. He saw himself dog-paddling around Mordy's big head, frightened at first and throwing his jaw back as though to touch the water with his chin would mean a certain death. He'd gasped then and choked at the thought of water filling his lungs, afraid to cry because those few extra drops of water from his eyes might just be enough to raise the river above his mouth. But soon, with Mordy's patient, guiding hands and kind words, Josef gained enough confidence to raise one hand out of the water and wave at his Aunt Lois, who smiled from a rock on shore. Then it wasn't long before Josef was doing the crawl, the breaststroke, even the backstroke. He'd swim races with Mordy, his aunt making the sound of the starter's pistol. He'd win, too. He became the fastest swimmer in his entire grade school hands down, though some of the kids did not take kindly to being beat and thought they ought to remind Josef of his scrawniness by wrestling him and bloodying his nose afterward.

Now here he was again, walking the beach with a bloody nose, as though he couldn't get away from it, as though there would always be someone to come around and remind him of his mortality and his weaknesses, usually just when he'd boosted his confidence by proving something else. But what could stop him now? As far as he knew, there was nothing between here and Biscayne but sun and sand. If he made the trip once, he knew he could do it indefinitely. If he didn't make it, he'd have no one to blame but himself.

The ocean rolled gently and shimmered now with scattered rays of sunlight. He let the warm water run up around his feet and splash the cuffs of his trousers. A few fiddler crabs dashed in arcs along the dunes, waving their oversized claws at Josef—like angry Brooklyn street vendors, he thought—before squeezing themselves into their holes for the day. A thin line of seaweed marked the highest advance of the tide, like a battle line drawn in a history book. There were dozens of little sandpipers to check the advance of the opposing army; periodic offensives would push them back up the beach, but always the pipers would contain the aggression and send the waves retreating—the ocean would never be entirely defeated, but its imperialist urges could be controlled.

Josef saw this action as a metaphor for man's role in nature. Nature could never, *should* never be defeated, he thought, but it was the duty of mankind to hold its sometimes-malevolent forces in check. Nature was a wild beast to be tamed for the benefit of man and God. It filled Josef's heart with an exultant sense of purpose to know that he was now playing a part in man's progress toward that goal.

This was his destiny, it seemed, the destiny of the torch-bearer, to keep the beacon of civilization glowing even in the remotest wilds. He was a link, as the postmaster had said, but more than just a link in the postal chain. He was the only link to civilization for an entire community of settlers who might otherwise be lost and forgotten, their bold experiment in hope and progress left unreported if not for him. This was the highest duty a man could aspire to, he thought.

The rolling surf and the early sun were so peaceful, and Josef had so much time to walk and think—he felt he had more time now than he'd ever had in his life, as if time had slowed to a near standstill here—that his mind began to wander far into the future, to the implications of this day and the fulfillment of this solemn task, handed to him like both a gift and a challenge from Above. He and other pioneers just like him were at the forefront of mankind's march into destiny. They were cutting the path and bearing the torches through the dark wild night and into the dawn, where wonderful things awaited them. Could it be, he thought, that this glorious land called Florida was truly the paradise of Eden, lost once through idle lust, but destined to be regained through the hard work of men like himself who humbled themselves before a higher goal?

What would such a paradise be like? Man can certainly not improve upon the perfection of God, he thought. It would have to resemble in every way the Eden of the Bible. Yet this Eden would be arrived at through the efforts of man. It would be an exact, man-made replication of Paradise. The New Paradise. The entire history of man would then be seen as a reconstruction of this Edenic framework. It had all been a learning process for the recreation of a single, beautiful, and perfect expression of God. Only then would man truly know and understand something of His nature.

He thought again of his swimming lessons. He'd seen his

uncle's demonstrations of the proper strokes and he'd heard his uncle's words describing to him the feeling and the techniques for propelling oneself through water. But never could Josef have imagined fully what the experience was until he replicated his uncle's movements himself. Of course it was not the same expression as Mordy's, but a near-exact replication of it. In this way, that experience of learning—indeed, every experience of learning—Josef now saw as an allegory of man's striving to return to Paradise, of his desire to replicate the Primary Gesture. Josef's endeavor was but a tiny step in that process—an arching of the elbow or a cupping of the hand to pull back the water—but it was an important one nonetheless. How many men or women had lived knowing they had played a part? The knowledge was a blessing in itself.

Josef saw before him the world of the future, where whole communities rose up out of the Florida jungle, and men and women lived in great comfort and ease as never before, as carefree as lambs romping across the dunes, soothed by the voice of the sea, or perhaps strolling blissfully through the flat green fields they'd carved out of the once-forbidding wilderness. For Nature had been thoroughly tamed. It had been molded into the harmonious patterns and pure designs of men in touch with their pure hearts, hearts that beat with God. Through his purity of purpose, man had become a conduit between God and Nature, rippling forth the patterns of the Heavens into the Wilds, imposing waves of Order onto the Chaos. Once perfected, the order of the Heavens would be the order of Nature. Man would have held a mirror up to the skies and reflected what he saw onto his own small world.

For the first time that day, Josef broke a sweat, and he wiped his brow. How long had he been thinking like this? It suddenly seemed too long, and he thought he'd better stop before he overstepped his bounds. Who was he, after all, to guess at the will of the Lord? Still, it was this feeling of duty, of working toward something dangerous even to imagine, that filled him with exhilaration and kept him going through the long, hot hours ahead.

For it wasn't long before the clouds dried up and crumbled apart, and the morning began to swelter. Before the sun had risen thirty degrees, Josef was tasting the drops of his sweat and his step had lost its initial jauntiness. His shirt began to collapse inward like a new weight on his skin. The three small straps around his neck—the postal sack, the lunch sack, and the canteen—seemed to add to their weight with each step, as though the distance he traveled was itself an invisible burden. His shoulders and back lost their sprightliness and sank accordingly. As his body sank, so did his thoughts—it was no longer so easy to look to the skies with high-minded thoughts of the future, for above him rose the sun, burning with rage as if it had read his thoughts about taming nature. Or perhaps it was only laughing.

Worst of all, the sand began to heat as rapidly as an iron skillet, and as it did so its whiteness brightened until it became not a color at all, but a light itself that pierced Josef's dry eyes from every direction. He could close his eyes for steps at a time, but he could not walk on air, and thus with every step his feet felt the hot, unrelenting grinding of the sand, which seemed to peel away the skin, layer by layer, bringing the heat to epidermal regions unused to and offended by such exposure. This was a pain he hadn't imagined possible in his feet—a region of the body so remote as to have seemed to him practically noncorporeal. Now these feet were very much a part of him, and very real in their pain. Despite months of working in his orchards, these were still the soft, uncalloused feet of a Brooklynite.

Almost as soon as his vision of Paradise had perfected itself in his mind, it had begun to evaporate and retreat. He could no longer grasp the beauty and perfection he'd just understood. The harmonious whole had quickly shredded itself into scraps. He saw only obstacles now, and his faith in man's ability to overcome them was shaken ever so slightly. How could this truly be Paradise, he thought, until man finds a way to cool the air? But Josef's overheated brain could not satisfactorily work out a solution. He thought of ferrying in huge icebergs from the Arctic. He thought of huge fans to redirect the wind from the North. But what was to prevent the icebergs from melting before they reached their destination? And who was to operate such gigantic fans? Would mankind have to redesign itself, too, in order to be comfortable in the overpowering heat and burdensome humidity of this New Paradise? It suddenly seemed beyond comprehension, and thus difficult to believe with complete faith. He had been given a beautiful and perfect vision of the Paradise to come, only to have it torn away by something as trivial as his bodily discomfort. What did that say about him?

He moved down the beach and walked along the shoreline, where the waves could cool his feet. With the sun not yet quite overhead, he decided he'd better rest. He still had many miles to go. There was no sense in wearing himself out.

He dragged himself up the dune with a singleness of purpose and crawled into a little clearing beneath the sea grapes. It was cooler there, and the change in temperature put him to sleep for a full hour, until the sun had risen directly above him and the cool shade evaporated.

His throat was brittle; it hurt to breathe too deeply. He put the canteen to his lips, then jerked his head back when the metal burned him. Half the water spilled out onto the sand. Then he ate one of the hot, dry fish fillets and began to peel a warm grapefruit when he heard a noise rustling in the palmetto bushes behind him. There was a flash of gray, and suddenly a wild boar was bearing down on him, tusks glistening with reflected sunshine.

Josef dropped the grapefruit and ran for shore, having only time to pull his mail sack with him. Grunts and snorts ringing in his ears, he dashed into the water holding the mail sack above his head so as not to soak its contents with his frenzied splashing. The water was to his waist when he finally stopped.

He turned around and there was the huge, ugly gray boar standing midway up the beach, pawing the sand like a bull and holding Josef's grapefruit in its mouth.

The boar snorted, pacing back and forth in nervous little jumps, keeping an eye on Josef, who now and then splashed at it with one hand, and shouted "Ya! Ya!" hoping to frighten it off. This only angered it more, and it would charge down to the very edge of the water, retreating only when a wave broke at its feet. Josef's heart seemed to beat in his throat. Standing there in the hot ocean, blinded by the reflected sunlight and holding the mail sack above his head, he had never felt more foolish and uncomfortable in his life.

After what seemed like hours, but was really only minutes, the boar turned its back and showed Josef its curly pigtail as it headed up the dune and into the bush, where Josef had left his food and water.

It was another long wait until the grunts trailed off and Josef felt it was safe enough to come out of the water. Nervously, he peeked under the sea grapes, and found the boar gone. And with it his food. The beast had even been malicious enough to spill the rest of the water out of his canteen.

Josef took a deep breath. He still had a day and a half of traveling to reach Biscayne. He began to walk again, slowly and soberly. What did he think now of the New Paradise? There was this problem of the beasts to contend with. It was clear that this place was full of malevolent creatures. They would have to be tamed like the land. They would have to do their part or stay out of the way.

He was thirsty and hungry and this made his indignation rankle. Animals, he thought, should not be allowed to stand in the way of man's salvation. Those who would submit to man's will and high purpose would be allowed a spot in Eden. But those like the boar who were full of the pride and fury of Satan would have to be locked up in cages and fences, living monuments to the triumph of good over evil.

A graceful row of seagulls passed overhead. Josef returned

their gaze suspiciously. He wondered what might lurk in the hearts of these creatures, which had always seemed good-natured. Were their cries a scornful malediction of humankind? Was the release of their excrement timed solely by biological need?

These thoughts, though painful to his moral sense, actually provided some momentary relief to his physical pain. But it wasn't long before his feet made themselves known again. Their tops were raw and beet-colored. He tried to pack a layer of wet sand over them, but the sun now burned in all its mid-afternoon fury; the white sand had become a crackling griddle that cooked his soles alive, and he had to walk in the water, which washed away any covering he could think of to put over his feet.

His trousers were soaked with seawater and his shirt soaked in sweat. Both clung to his skin like a clammy film of seaweed. They weighed him down, but he dared not remove anything for fear of the sun. His pace slowed dramatically and his gait became more erratic. His breathing became labored and noisy. The very act of seeing, of moving, of sensing his world, became a painful curse he'd renounce in an instant had he the energy to speak the words. Instead, he moved forward, trance-like, with only a small ray of hope that it would all end soon.

At last, in late afternoon, he came upon an inlet, and this gave him an excuse to rest. The inlet provided a half-mile-wide estuary where creatures of the river and creatures of the sea came face to face, eyeing one another like beings from opposite worlds. Then there were the rare creatures like the manatee, caught between both worlds, not fully a part of either. If Josef had retained the ability to think clearly, he might have identified himself at that moment with those gentle outcasts, for he could not help but feel trapped between worlds, unable to return to Brooklyn without shame, yet seemingly unable to make his way through the rigors of this new environment.

There was a small skiff on shore that the postmaster had mentioned, with *Property of the United States Postal Service* and a small postal insignia painted on either side. With the little strength he had left, he pushed off and began to row across the inlet. Shortly, though, he dropped the oars and reclined in the boat, the mail sack falling to his side. The air was beginning to cool, and the gentle rocking made him drowsy. The day had grown silent, with only the soft slap of the water at the sides of his boat to send him off to sleep.

He drifted there in the estuary, in the space between two worlds, wholly unaware of a new predicament: it was high tide, and all around him, a feeding frenzy had begun. Dozens of alligators, who care nothing about whether a meal tastes salty or fresh, had moved up river to the inlet to feed on the convergence of fish. The gators snapped at the water, stuck their snouts up and swallowed whatever happened to fall across their razored jaws. The sea churned with blood, fish leapt in every direction. But none of this stirred Josef, whose head rested on the edge of the skiff, dangerously close to the snapping gators. Not even when gators knocked the boat and bit at it as they bit at everything else in their paths, not even when the silvery fish jumped into his boat to escape, then jumped back out to accept their fate—not even then did Josef stir from his much-deserved sleep.

Chapter 10

SOMETHING LANDED ON Josef's chest, and he reached down to brush it off. A moment later, something bigger seemed to land there, and he grunted, still half-asleep, and brushed this one away, too. It came back again, though, heavier this time and thumping his chest as it landed. Now Josef jerked his head up off its wooden pillow and moved to squash the creature once and for all.

But when he opened his eyes he found he'd grabbed not a bug, but the wrist of a man. The man was young and dark and wore a knee-length skirt and colorful patchwork shirt. He stood half a step back from the boat and, bending forward, he clasped Josef's wrist in reciprocation, shaking it up and down and smiling as if Josef had just been initiated into an exclusive club.

It was Josef's first encounter with an Indian, and before he had time to think anything else, all the monstrous tales about violent, savage cannibals leapt into his thoughts, and he pushed himself up in the boat, knocking his head against a mangrove branch. As if to confirm Josef's fears, the Indian wiped the smile off his own face and drew a knife from his belt. He held the knife to Josef's face, twisting it back and forth between his thumb and forefinger. He still held Josef's wrist with his other hand.

"What do you want?" said Josef, pulling the mail sack tightly to his side.

The Indian smiled again, seeing Josef was properly scared. He was a little taller than Josef, and had pudgy cheeks and black hair parted in the middle. He let go of Josef's wrist and, still standing back from the boat and careful not to touch the sides of it, he reached across with his knife hand and poked the sole of Josef's right foot, which was still propped up on the boat bench.

Josef felt nothing but fear, since his foot was asleep. He tried to pull it in, at least get it off the bench, but to no avail.

The Indian prodded Josef's toes again and then let out a laugh, pointing at Josef with his knife, throwing his head back and showing his big yellow teeth.

Finally, Josef's leg began to make itself known, and he grabbed it in pain and pushed it to the floor of the boat. This sudden gesture startled the Indian, and he reached into the boat, still careful not to touch the edge, and yanked Josef out of it with surprising strength. For the first time, Josef realized he was onshore beside the inlet. He could not remember exactly how he'd gotten across it.

The Indian motioned with his knife and turned him toward a path through the mangrove swamp. Josef felt a little shove in that direction, but as he started forward, he noticed for the first time something odd on the Indian's feet. He'd always thought of Indian men in loincloths and bare feet. But here was a man in a skirt whose feet fit snugly into a pair of black leather boots up to mid-calf. And there were rows and designs of pebbles and shells pasted all over them.

Josef didn't have much time to think about this, though. With a hand on his shoulder, the Indian guided him down a twisting, low-ceilinged path. His legs and feet were stiff and aching, but he was glad to be in the shade.

They trudged through some shallow swamp water and soon arrived at a small village on some high ground surrounded on all sides by swamp. The path led directly between

93

two rows of thatched huts, most without walls and held up by a single pole in the center. There were cooking fires burning and smoke rising up out of the mangroves.

Josef's captor called to some of the other Indians in a language Josef couldn't comprehend, and several young men came running to the path. They, too, wore leather boots, and when they approached Josef, they looked down at his bare feet and laughed. He couldn't help but be a bit self-conscious. Why were his feet so uproariously funny to them? He tightened his grip on the postal sack; it felt now like a security blanket for him, a token of civilization among these savages.

People began to shout all over the camp, announcing the presence of the stranger. As they dashed out toward him from under their huts, Josef couldn't help noticing all of their boots. It seemed that all of the men above puberty had fine-looking leather boots on their feet, some black, others brown, and all decorated with shells, stones, and sometimes feathers. It was obvious that some did not fit their owners properly, that they'd not yet grown into them or had grown too big for them, so that many of them seemed to stumble over them as they walked, or else take small, gingerly steps with stalwart grimaces on their faces. The children were all barefoot, but some of the women wore boots, too, though not as elaborately decorated as the men's. Still, even the barefoot members of the tribe could not contain their laughter at Josef's feet, and Josef suddenly felt he'd exposed something private and shameful.

He was led into one of the walled huts and up to an elderly man sitting on a small stool and clothed in a colorful knee-length dress, silver jewelry, small animal skins dangling from his headwear and belt, and the most elaborately decorated boots of the tribe. Josef understood this to be the chief. His boots were so completely covered with shells and stones they looked rock stiff and impossible to walk in. Perhaps this explained why the chief did not leave his stool to greet Josef.

Other elders poured into the room, having gotten wind of Josef's presence. They stood behind the chief, and Josef was separated from the group by a large bucket of water in the center of the room. Behind him were curious commoners, as many as could squeeze themselves into the room without crossing the invisible line that divided them from the elders. Those who could not get in the room stuck their heads through the doors and windows and jostled for a glimpse of the stranger.

The chief gave a sign and everyone but Josef immediately sat down on the dirt floor, the elders on woven rugs. Some words were spoken and several young women emerged from the crowd carrying palm fronds. They sat between Josef and the bucket of water and waved the fronds over the top of it, circulating cooler air inside the hut. Josef was startled at the simplicity and ingenuity of this air-cooling device, and wondered, strange as it might seem, if these Indians were also working toward rebuilding Paradise. They seemed to have long ago recognized the problem Josef had made note of only yesterday, and they'd already developed this simple technique for solving it. Josef wondered how this could be implemented on a grander scale. Perhaps he'd found a place for these people in the New Paradise. A thousand of them at once could be sent just offshore loaded up with big palm fronds that they'd fan vigorously over the ocean, thereby creating a cool ocean breeze for those on land. What a masterful plan, he thought. Not only would the air be permanently cooled, but all those floating rafts would serve as a barrier reef to break up the bigger Atlantic waves; between the shore and the fan-rafts would be nothing but glassy green lagoon.

The chief eyed Josef carefully. Then he signaled for a young brave to sit between him and Josef on the equatorial line marked by the bucket.

"Español?" asked the brave.

Josef shook his head.

After speaking with the chief, another young brave was brought in to replace the first.

"English?" he asked.

95

Josef shook his head proudly. "American," he said.

A third interpreter was brought forth out of the crowd.

"Yank," he said.

Josef nodded.

The chief looked at Josef and spoke in a musical, vowel-laden tongue.

The interpreter listened, then turned to Josef.

"Why do you disgrace your people?" he said, speaking in an accent no worse than Josef's. "Have they cast you out?"

"I don't understand," said Josef.

"Your feet. They are as bare as a child's or an unmarried woman's. It is shameful to look at."

The chief turned his head away, refusing to look at Josef for a moment. Then a woman behind him brought forth a blanket and covered Josef's feet.

Now the chief spoke again, and the interpreter did his work.

"Your swollen face and your bare feet show us that your people have scorned you. Yet whatever crime you have committed, they have not felt you worthy of a proper execution. And so neither do we. You are doomed to shame yourself as you walk the land, for we will not provide you even with sandals. Leave our sight."

Josef was pulled back by the armpits.

"Wait!" said the interpreter, at the chief's command. "Leave your sack. You must pay us something for bringing your disgrace to our village."

Josef grasped the strap of the mail sack with both hands. "I cannot," he said.

Some strong braves behind him yanked it out of his hands and threw it across the bucket to the chief. He inspected it carefully. When he turned it over, he saw the postal insignia and dropped the sack in front of him, gasping.

The elders crowded around, leaning over the chief and looking down at the sack. There were assenting small gasps, echoing the chief's.

Even the interpreter looked over at the bag and swallowed deeply. "You are government," he said. "Why do you keep this a secret?"

"It is no secret," said Josef. "I am a United States Postal Carrier."

The chief spoke. "Take your sack," said the interpreter. "We may not touch it. We have been told by the white man. His gods forbid us to touch anything where the Great Eagle has left its mark."

Dozens of eyes watched as Josef stepped over and picked up his mail sack, then returned to his spot. The chief looked at Josef with fear and utter amazement. He conferred with the other elders for a moment, and a heated conversation broke out among them.

Finally, the chief addressed Josef again.

"Tell us for true," said the interpreter. "Are you a real white man?"

"I am," said Josef.

"We have heard that Indians who touch the mark of the Great Eagle may turn white forever. We suspect you are one of the braves lost in the great storm of last year. We suspect you saved yourself by clinging to the boat of the Great Eagle, but now you are doomed to be a white man."

Josef remembered the young brave's reluctance to touch any part of the Postal Service boat. "No," he said. "I am a white man from Brooklyn. I don't know your people or customs."

"Then how do you explain your uncovered feet?" At this, a woman reached over and covered Josef's feet again, for the blanket had fallen away.

"We think the white man discovered your true nature and sent you away from their village without shoes. We know that the white man thinks our people walk without shoes, because we used to wear buckskin sandals, which the white man does not recognize as shoes. Perhaps this is why the white man thinks badly of us and wants to make war with us. But those days are over. We can no longer make war with the white man. We can only try to keep what's left of our lands and our home. Many of our tribe have agreed to leave this land and live in the lands to the distant west, but our small group and perhaps some others have decided to remain, even if it means adapting to some of the white man's ways. Not long after we cast ourselves out from the rest of the tribe, we came upon the wreckage of one of the white man's boats. There were many crates cast up on the beach, and when we opened them we found the leather boots you see us wear today. We took this gift as a sign from our own gods that we were now to start wearing boots so the white man will respect us and our lands. Of course, we could not resist enriching their design with our own style. But you wear nothing. So you must have disgraced yourself among the white men."

"No," said Josef. "It's because of one white man only that I do not wear shoes." And suddenly inspired, he lost all his nervousness and told them the whole story of his childhood in Austria, of his coming to America, of his aunt and uncle and even his wife and their failed efforts to grow citrus in Figulus, and finally of his uncle's death and the missing pair of loafers. "And so," he concluded, "it is in honor of my deceased Uncle Mordy, who raised me as a son, that I have made this personal decision to walk my mail route barefoot."

Josef waited while the interpreter paraphrased the entire tale for the chief. When it was over, the Indians broke out in great laughter.

It took a few minutes for the chief to regain his composure and address Josef again.

"We do not know if you are a red man or a white man, but we know now that you are a fool."

Josef's face turned a shade darker than any Indian's face. There was a brief silence and they all seemed to study him as a curiosity.

"You are all mixed up. You seek to do your fathers an honor. This is the way of the red man; this is good. And yet you shame yourself in doing so, exposing your feet to laughter and the anger of the sun, who surely finds your gesture offensive. This is the way of white men, the way of fools. We think you do not know who you are."

Josef had nothing to say in his defense. The elders conferred again.

The interpreter summed up the results of the conference. "By handing the chief the sack of the Great Eagle, you have exposed our tribe to dangers. The chief fears he might turn white. Or that the entire tribe will turn white. We must know your true nature so we can perform some precautionary rituals. The Great Eagle may have affected your head so that you no longer remember whether you are white or red. Yet you tell long stories about your white past. We question the truth of these stories. It may be that you know you were once one of us, and you are angered that you cannot return to the tribe of your blood, so you take out your anger on all red men   you seek to change us all into white. Our prophets have told us that one day the Great Eagle may swoop down from the skies, and as the tips of his wings touch us, one by one, we will all turn white, and our tribe and all of our history—our honor and our bravery, even our gods—will be forgotten forever. If you are the Great Eagle, we want you to have pity on us and tell us right now, so that we may kiss our wives and hold our children one last time before our memories are wiped clean."

A flash of guilt illumined Josef's mind to the injustice of his previous thoughts. If the Indians were to wave their fronds and cool the inhabitants of Paradise, who would cool the Indians? He hadn't thought of their well-being; he hadn't thought of them as full-fledged humans. But now he understood something of their plight and wondered whether certain animals could be trained to float behind the Indians and wave palm fronds to cool them as they cooled the white men on shore. Mules came to mind. Dogs, perhaps. But they would have to be bred big to hold the branches in their jaws all day. He didn't have time to think it through now.

"I swear that I'm no Great Eagle," he said. "I mean you no

harm. I wish only to make prompt delivery of this sack and fulfill my duty to my government and my people."

Another short conference took place among the elders.

"Your words have the sound of truth, man of unknown color. Still, we must be certain because the consequences of a deception could mean the end of our tribe. We must detain you here and observe you to see what blood runs in your veins."

Everyone stood again, and Josef was led through the throng of curious Indians, which split to give him a wide berth. Though all but the very youngest of them had seen white people before, they were strangely fascinated by Josef. His face was still frighteningly swollen from his debacle in the postmaster's restaurant. And his hair was darker than most other white men's hair, his skin not quite so pale; to many people in the tribe, here was visual evidence that he'd once been one of them.

They spoke amongst themselves, bringing up names of men who'd disappeared from their tribe, but whose bodies had never been recovered. They examined Josef's face, trying to decide which of their tribe lay under that puffy mask. Some thought it was Yaha-Chatee, the man who was lost in the great storm. Others thought it was Tustenuggee, the man who had disappeared in the river, whom they thought had been eaten by alligators. Still another faction agreed it was Emathla, the young scout who couldn't wait until he'd grown up to explore the swamp, who one day twenty years ago had toddled out of his mother's hut and into the wilderness forever. Or so they'd thought.

As Josef passed through the crowd, they shouted these names at him—"Yaha!" "Tuste!" and "Emathla!"—each faction hoping they could prove their theory by Josef's reaction. Several members of the Emathla group felt that Josef had turned his head slightly at the sound of that name, but the other factions only laughed and said that the Emathla people had their eyes pointed at the backs of their heads and could only see the little pictures their brains made for them. They all laughed at each other, but they no longer laughed at Josef, because now that they looked at him closely, his blackened eyes and his swollen nose indeed gave him the appearance of an eagle, and his disgraceful bare feet suddenly took on mystical and cataclysmic qualities.

He was taken to a walled, unoccupied hut. As the crowd lingered outside, he was given a mat and told to sit down. They watched his motions carefully, especially the way he sat on the mat. A great bucket of cool water, like the one in the chief's hut, was brought in and placed in the middle of the floor. Soon after, a trio of women appeared. Two of them carried bowls of food—some soup, meat, and fruit—while the third presented him with a steaming black drink, darker than coffee.

He was left alone, then, though he could see the skirts of two braves stationed outside his door, and passersby could not help but pause for a glimpse of the white Indian until the braves waved them off.

He was still too nervous to eat, but his lips and throat ached from the salty air. He sniffed the pungent black drink, which smelled of ginseng and a dozen other bitter herbs and roots he could not identify. He tried to sip it and his entire mouth seemed to tighten and collapse of its own accord. A shiver ran down his spine, and the small amount of liquid that squeezed itself down his throat felt like it was building a railroad as it went. He took a few bites of grapefruit just to wash it down.

Then he took a good look around him for the first time and spotted the reason he'd been given this hut. There was a small hole in the thatched wall, and someone had his eye to it, observing him, studying him. The eye saw him looking and moved away from the peephole. Josef turned his back to it. *So that's it*, he thought; *I'm to be studied like a caged animal. My behavior is to be noted and weighed as evidence in some kind of experiment.*

Josef pondered his dilemma. If their changeling theory was proved correct, then he might be forced to remain with the tribe and "rehabilitated." He couldn't let that happen; he had a duty to the U.S. Postal Service and the nation at large to get his mail sack delivered, not to mention a duty to himself and his uncle to carry out his big plans as a pioneer. If he were somehow able to disprove their theory, he'd risk being seen as their destroyer and, though they'd probably think it would do no good in the long run, they'd want to kill him on the spot, on the slim chance that the Great Eagle was mortal or at least able to be wounded. Yet he could not think of a way to prove he was white.

He clutched the canvas mail sack in his hands, praying for guidance.

Soon some of the elders entered his hut and sat opposite him. There was no interpreter; they'd just come to observe. They studied the remains of the grapefruit he'd taken some bites of, inspecting the way he'd peeled off the skin, and the size and depths of his bites. One man held the meat in front of Josef's nose, and Josef turned away, recognizing the smell of alligator meat that brought back painful memories from the postmaster's restaurant.

The elders exchanged looks, each of them thinking, *Yes, this is white man's behavior, but neither did Yaha-Chatee favor the taste of alligator meat.* Still, they could certainly rule out Tustenuggee, since he'd have eaten his own mother, had she been a gator. Of course, Tuste had been a tremendous jokester; if this white man was truly Tustenuggee he'd be lying for the simple pleasure of lying. Clearly, more tests were needed.

The elders left to consult with the chief, and they left Josef alone for the rest of the day, which Josef occupied with thoughts of his dear Lena. He slept little that night, for whenever he opened his eyes, there was that peephole, and though he could not definitely make out a staring eye, the hole seemed far too dark for a moonlit night.

WHEN THE ELDERS returned in the morning, they brought with them two braves who carried bows and arrows. Josef was led out of his hut, and the group traveled down a damp path out of the village and through the swamp to a cleared plot of high ground. Josef's legs trembled as he walked; he thought he was being taken to his death. *And what a terrible way to die!* he thought. His body would be thrown into the swamp by these red men, and he'd never be heard from again. The mail would go undelivered and his wife and aunt back in Brooklyn would never get word of him. His great plans would go unrealized, the small progress he'd made thus far would be forgotten. He'd not even warrant a footnote in the great struggle to rebuild Paradise.

When they came to a stop on the island, the elders spoke and the two braves loaded their bows. Josef's heart raced and his hands shook. He tasted the black drink returning to his throat. He closed his eyes, waiting for the end. But nothing happened. When he opened them again, he saw an opossum emerge from beside a mangrove some sixty feet away. The braves took careful aim, and an instant later the opossum was on its side, two arrows side by side in its neck.

The braves congratulated each other with a handshake. Josef wondered if this was to be his last supper—a filthy opossum eaten in the company of Indians.

Instead, one of the braves handed him his bow and an arrow, and the other brave tried to demonstrate how to use them. The elders observed gravely.

Somehow, Josef got the arrow loaded properly on the bow. His hands shook wildly. He knew his performance could mean the difference between life and death. Yet he didn't know whether he preferred life as a captive to these Indians or an inglorious death at their hands. He didn't have time to think about it, for now another opossum showed its pink nose. Josef couldn't help but think this animal, too, had the heart of Satan, and he prayed that the opossum, along with the boar, would be excluded from Paradise, just as they'd done all in their power to exclude him from his role in its construction.

Josef pulled the bow back as far as he could, which wasn't even half as far as the braves had done. The bow shuddered in his hands. He closed his eyes, and a moment later something hit him in the back of the head. He thought he'd felt his last earthly sensation.

But again, he opened his eyes and knew he was alive. He lay on the spongy earth, the bow resting on his chest, looking straight up into a tree, where the arrow he'd fired hung loosely from a tree branch.

The braves couldn't keep from laughing as they helped him to his feet. The elders thought, *Very convincing white man's behavior, even for Yaha-Chatee. But it could be Emathla, since he disappeared while he was still too young to know the Way of the Arrow. Tustenuggee was a superior marksman, but this raises a new question: is it a man's blood or his skin that determines his excellence in arrow shooting? Perhaps Tustenuggee lost his ability to shoot when his skin paled. If so, then is there a proportional relationship between arrow-shooting ability and skin color, or is there a critical shading of skin below which a man cannot possibly achieve arrow-shooting excellence?*

The elders were intrigued. They agreed that once this man's blood had been determined, they would call together all the best arrow shooters of the tribe and take measurements of their skin color to see if the two were positively correlated. *Perhaps some day,* thought one, *we can match up men and women of the darkest skin color, thus producing a breed of the greatest warriors the tribe has ever known. Perhaps then the white men will run scared, and all of the tribe's enemies will be defeated with great ease.* As they walked back to the village, the elders pondered the exciting possibilities.

The elders remained in Josef's tent the rest of the afternoon and into the evening, studying him closely, speaking few words among themselves, and no words at all to Josef. With the men watching, Josef ate very little of his supper, some sort of thick gray stew with chunks of fish. Whenever he took a bite, the men would point at him and make comments, "a-ha" noises, and even quiet laughter. Josef had never felt more self-conscious in his life. Before the bowl was taken out of the hut, the elders huddled around it to inspect exactly how much he'd eaten and which of the vegetables and fish he'd eaten the most of. Worst of all, when they let him out of the hut to relieve himself, Josef thought he spotted someone watching him in the woods; and when he'd finished and headed back to the hut, he was certain there was someone poking around where he'd been, taking samples for later analysis.

The elders left his hut when it began to grow dark, but they weren't finished with their experiments, for shortly after, a young squaw entered alone. Her dark skin and deep black eyes and hair reminded Josef of the tales he'd heard about native women in the South Pacific who drove dedicated seamen to heinous mutinies and greedy traders to abandon their business.

At first, the girl merely sat across from him and waved a palm frond over the water bucket to cool him. Josef thought the idea was for him to get some rest in preparation for another day of experimentation and close observation. The breeze she made with the palm frond was cool and refreshing, like the first breath of autumn that settled the dust and the tempers in the Brooklyn marketplace. His weariness at last overcoming his fears, he lowered himself to his side and closed his eyes.

He dozed off, and soon began to dream of a reunion with Lena. Back in Brooklyn, her cares would be few. There'd be nothing to trouble her mind and make her curl up in a distressed little ball at night, unresponsive to Josef's affections. She'd open her arms to him unbegrudgingly, forgiving in a single gesture all that had come between them, all of his foolish plans and his pathetic failures and the dangers and discomforts to which he'd subjected her. Then at last their marriage would be consummated and all that had happened between the day of their wedding and the day of their consummation would be erased from their lives, as though it had never happened, as though he'd sent a letter to himself on his wedding day and, though the letter had traveled for months, down to Florida and back again, in the end there was nothing to mark the distance it had traveled or all the hands it had passed through but a simple postmark, and the time that had elapsed between would be collapsed into sheer, beautiful nothingness.

It all seemed so real and possible to Josef that he thought he felt his wife's hands caressing his chest as he slept. She was nudging him, desiring his attentions, but still too bashful to tell him outright, he thought. He need not say anything, just reach for her hand, hold it in his, open his eyes and smile at the woman he loved. Or perhaps it was better not to look at her yet; he didn't wish to embarrass her. Soon enough, she'd grow bold, and he'd find her astride his stomach, her beautiful naked body gleaming with twilight.

Yes, things would be well then, he could open his eyes and look deeply into hers. She'd slide his nightshirt off and massage oils onto his chest in slow, gentle circles, her small firm breasts only inches from his nose, and he'd reach up and hold them lovingly, smiling at this sexually playful, almost aggressive side to her he could never have imagined in the early days of their marriage. And yes, he could look at her then and see the love in her eyes. Just when he thought he could no longer bear the intensity of his desire he'd find himself shrouded in the deepest miracle of feeling that nature had to offer. And he'd let his body break into what felt like a million separate fragments of disconnected sensation, for each part of him to experience that feeling individually. They'd fall together again on their own, into a wholeness that seemed to make him more alive than the sum of all his parts. Like a breathing motion, the experience would repeat itself perfectly, and it dawned on him then that this was the gentle breath of Paradise, repeating itself since In the Beginning, like an echo that does not fade, waiting to be acknowledged by someone like himself, and here he was like a Chosen One, accepting this gift and the knowledge of its supreme importance, the breath that would breathe life into his God-given Vision of Paradise. And all he had to do was open his eyes and bathe himself in the light of God, the light that was the eyes and the future of all mankind.

The breathing grew stronger then, until the world itself seemed nothing but breathing, each breath quicker and stronger than the last, and each time more and more of himself flying forth and investing itself into the individual fragments that seemed to conjoin with the breath of God, and taking longer and longer to pull himself back into a whole, each time losing just a little bit of the mortar that held him together, until he thought, *If I let go this time, I'll no longer be Josef Steinmetz, but a thousand particles of perfect and joyful beatitude scattered into the infinite breath of God.* At that very moment, every sensation Josef had ever felt conjoined into one and released itself in an explosive sensation the likes of which he'd never imagined possible, and in the vacuum created by that explosion, the fragments of himself were pulled all at once back into the center, in great disarray at first, but then gently and painlessly returning to their natural geometry.

Only then did he open his eyes and see the face of the squaw.

She wore no expression whatsoever and pushed herself off him, and when he looked up at her, he was reminded of that moment earlier in the day when he thought he'd died, only to open his eyes to the misfired arrow dangling from the branch above him, making a cruel joke of his fear and sadness.

The squaw dressed and left, but Josef could not watch her go. He could not turn his head; he hadn't the will. *I was asleep*, he thought, *and cruelly taken advantage of for the sake of these pagan superstitions.* But there was this nagging feeling that he hadn't been fully asleep, that maybe he'd known what was going on, and had let his baser desires get the best of him. He knew right then he'd never be able to fully convince himself of his innocence, and that if he ever tried to tell Lena, he'd falter terribly and make himself out to be more of a monster than even he considered himself at this very moment.

When he finally sat up, he looked across the room in the last light of day and saw the little peephole and the eye of an elder peering through it. And then he saw two more holes and two more unblinking eyes, and he wondered if he'd heard them making those holes, and had paid no attention, or worse, that the three eyes had only fueled the fire of his perversion and the lie he told himself with his eyes closed and his mind pretending to be with God.

Hollow and ashamed, Josef felt like crying, though he held it back with all his strength; those eyes at the peepholes had seen enough.

He held his head in his hands for what seemed like hours, until his morbid and self-pitying thoughts were interrupted by the sound of gunshots.

Chapter 11

SUDDENLY THE VILLAGE was in an uproar. There were shouts and screams and quick, heavy footsteps all around, everything quickened and intensified by the intermittent gunshots. At first Josef was just thankful to have something take his mind off what he'd done with the Indian woman. Then he thought that perhaps they'd reached a conclusion about his being the Great Eagle and now a ceremony had begun that would reach its climax with his slaughter. He felt utterly alone and unprotected.

There were heavy steps outside his door and then someone stepped inside. Josef couldn't even discern the outline of a figure, because now the moon was hidden by storm clouds; there were rumblings of an approaching storm.

"There a white man in 'ere?" said an English voice.

Josef was elated; here was the voice of civilization. "Yes! I am here! I am a white man!"

The voice called outside his hut, "'E's in 'ere! I got 'im!"

In a few moments, there was a commotion at the door and several men entered.

A hand grabbed Josef by the arm. "Come along wi' us. We'll save ya from these 'ere heathens." A flash of lightning illumined an aged and deeply lined face.

Josef was not undisturbed by the strange voices and the

grasping hands in the darkness, but he followed anyway, clutching his mail sack to his chest, glad to be moving forward again.

The Englishmen marched him through the village. Josef counted five different voices and discerned some of their figures when lightning flashed or when they passed near to a burning hut. They were big men. When they spotted an Indian scurrying to safety, they fired shots into the air. Josef sensed the Indians crouching in fear as they watched their huts burn. He felt sorry for them. There was something terrible and violent about these white men, and yet here they were saving his scalp.

They marched out of the village, leaving a narrow swath of terror and destruction, then followed an unseen path through the black swamp. It began to rain, and Josef was soaked all at once while he tried to protect his mail sack. None of the men seemed to mind. The man beside him kept his big hand around Josef's arm and spoke continuously—"Stupid bloody heathens. Black-booted boobies. Red-faced monkey scavengers. Yer all right now, I tell ya. Yer in good hands. We saved ya from their filthy animal paws. Yer fine now. Yer back t'civilization. Yer among friends. Why, jest a few minutes longer and you'd've taken a berlin' bubble bath, I tell ya. The bloody cannibals. Yer teeth woulder made fer some fancy garnish on the chief's boots. The gaudy, dress-wearin twits. Yer awright now. Yer back wid white men. We're all yer friends here. . . ."

Josef was soaked to the bone and chilled. The soft, cool mud of the swamp oozed up between his toes. He had a strange feeling about these men. They were nothing more than voices in the dark, and he wondered if they were truly leading him back to civilization. What if he were to return? How could he hold himself tall when he'd shamed himself with an Indian woman? How could he ever hope to face Lena again? He couldn't even imagine writing her a letter now, because the only proper words would be a complete confession, and he doubted his courage to write them.

Things were happening too quickly for his thoughts to keep up. Perhaps he was mistaken to leave the Indian village so eagerly. There may have been a kernel of truth in their changeling theory. For why else would he have given himself over to a squaw? In that moment, at least, he had become one of them. It seemed obvious now; he'd known what he was doing. The least he could do was have the courage to admit it to himself, if not to Lena: in his pioneer's desire to distance himself from the Old World and from those fancy Brooklyn avenues of his youth, he'd redefined his sensibilities completely and now found them cloaked in red. Perhaps it was a sign of madness. Surely Lena would think so. Yet anyone who'd felt what he felt when he'd coupled with that Indian woman would know that he'd found a new sense of purpose. He couldn't forget that. Lena would never understand; but she didn't know what he knew.

As usual, though, he'd reached his conclusions just a few moments too late. It seemed that he was forever being punished, that he was forever sampling the forbidden fruit and being turned out of Eden just as he'd learned to enjoy its delights. It occurred to him that he might build and rebuild his paradise a million times and never recognize it as the one true Eden. Perhaps he was destined to forever look his beloved in the eye and never know her true identity. He simply hadn't the purity of heart or the strength of will.

But another possibility presented itself to him. Perhaps he'd so confused himself that he'd regressed. Surely the Indian way to Paradise was the false way, the way of animals and heathens, for it wasn't a rebuilding of Paradise, but rather a return to the Paradise of old where humans and animals were alike in that they could know no shame. He'd given himself to that Indian woman as though he were little more than a beast with natural urges. In his weakness, perhaps he yearned for that lost innocence. He yearned to forget the taste of the fruit, and his scrambled thoughts did not recognize the impossibility of this.

Still, he couldn't deny the religious beauty of those moments with the squaw. That was something far greater than satisfying an urge. It was far greater than a carnal sin. It was the state of bliss, something man ought to strive for eternally, something that ought to be an integral component of any earthly paradise.

"Yer among yer kind, now," said the voice beside him again. "Yer safe, mate. The bloody heathens. We'll teach 'em a thing er two. . . ."

The thunder pounded in his ears and shook up his thoughts as he walked. He'd come so far from that protective lie of his father's and from the illusion of the wine labels that they suddenly seemed attractive again. He'd have given anything at that moment to erase all the time that had come between and return to his childhood in the Old World, pasting on those labels of the convent that didn't exist, believing the illusion that his family would be gathered like this forever, sitting around a tub of more wine bottles than they could ever hope to label, bonded together and blissful in their sense of duty. That was the vision of paradise that kept coming back to him now. That was the one he'd be forever trying to rebuild.

SOMETIME LATE IN the night the rain stopped, and they reached a small camp where a couple of other men sat around a fire, rifles cradled in their arms. For the first time, Josef got a good look at their faces. They were all craggy, sailor types, faces wizened before their time, with sparkling eyes and thick, dark beards that they pulled on as they talked. And there was one other that stood out from the rest because he was beardless, young, and fair haired. They called him Mick.

Josef was given a plate of stew, and, suddenly famished, he ate it as though his own mother had made it. It tasted familiar and safe. The men spoke in whispers amongst themselves, some occasionally raising their voices to shout, "The bloody bastard scavengers!" and someone else would fire his rifle in the air in agreement.

Josef didn't know who these men were. Perhaps they were a group of hunters from a nearby town he'd never heard of. Or perhaps they were mercenaries employed by the U.S. Government to control the remaining Indian population, ones who refused to go quietly into the reservations, ones like the group that had captured him. Or perhaps they really were pirates, though Josef hadn't thought such people existed anymore outside storybooks. Or, it now dawned on him, they might be the beach scavengers he'd read about in his guidebooks, groups who made their living off shipwrecks by killing the survivors and taking what remained of the ship's cargo. Sometimes, he'd read, they actually set signal fires, as though they themselves were shipwreck survivors, to draw the obliging Samaritans directly into a reef. Until now, he'd taken those stories for little more than local legends, perhaps based on truth, but enhanced to make the area seem more colorful. In any case, it appeared certain that Josef's rescue from the Indians was not altogether a positive development.

When he'd finished eating, Josef was led into a small tent where he collapsed into an uneasy sleep, using his wet postal sack for a pillow.

"Top o' the mornin," said the man who woke him. Josef recognized the voice of the man who'd held him by the arm the night before.

He pushed himself off the dirt floor.

"Don' look so frightened, friend. Come out and get ya some breakfast. We mean ya no harm."

Josef stepped out of the tent. Most of the men were gathered around the fire, eating.

"Looks's though them Injuns did the job on yer face, mate. We saved ya jest in time."

Someone handed Josef a tin plate. He stared at the crisp bacon and the deep brown sausage with amazement. He breathed in their rich and familiar aromas; he could think of no food more perfect and desirable.

113

A man laughed. "Arr. Surprise ya, does it? We eat finely here. You'll see, mate."

"We're blessed, we are," said another man. "The Good Lord provides us well."

"Aye. This bounty is heaven sent."

"Pushed ashore by His good hand, it was."

They laughed.

"I don't understand," said Josef.

"We're mere harvesters of the Lord's bounty, friend."

"And the Reaper's refuse."

They all laughed loudly, with such abandon that Josef shrunk back. They seemed to confirm his suspicions.

"Are you men scavengers?" he asked.

They stopped laughing and the man next to him gave him a hard shove, spilling Josef's plate.

"We ain't no scavengers, mate."

"I say we hang 'im for callin us so."

"I say we feed 'im to the sharks."

"We're simple beachcombers, that's what we is. Living off the Lord's generous gifts."

"Aye. What the Lord giveth, we hauleth away."

Laughter.

"Now, those bloody heathens we rescued ya from, *they're* scavengers. Bloody vultures, they are. And thieves."

Josef did not see the distinction. A shudder of fright renewed itself up his weakened spine. He reassured himself: there must be some reason they'd rescued him.

"Let's have a look at that little bag a yours." The man reached out to grab Josef's mail sack, but Josef held firm.

Josef's response was automatic, he'd been told what to say by the Figulus postmaster, and he'd repeated it over and over in his walk down the beach, a droning voice in the back of his head, in time with the hiss of his footsteps. He said, "This is property of the U.S. Government. Any tampering will result in prosecution under full penalty of law."

"Arr. I told ya, Frankie. This 'ere's the new mailboy."

Josef saw smiles break across their red, prunish faces.

"He'll net us a fortune," said the young one.

"Shut up, Mick," said another one. "This Yank's government property, 'e says. We don't want no trouble wi' the law, eh?"

"That's right, Tom. We're proper law abiders, we are."

"It's so. We'll treat this 'ere gov'ment property like it's our own."

"We will at that."

"We'll make inquiries, we will. See if the gov'ment cares to 'ave its property returned."

"Surely they will, Frankie. They've a gen'rous gov'ment here, they do. They like to keep their citizens smiling."

"Aye. An I b'lieve this gen'rous gover'ment'd be willin to reimburse us for his upkeep, don't you, Tom?"

"I do at that. Not so much, mind you. But a little somethin for our troubles. After all, we rescued 'im from the clutches of the enemy."

"Sure. It's a good thing we came upon that full-fleshed Injun squaw t'other day, and a good thing that squaw had a mind to tell us about the mailboy they'd got penned up in the village."

"Good thing we let her keep her throat to tell us, too."

"Shame about them others, though."

Josef had slipped from the grasp of Indians only to fall in with a group of murderous scavengers who meant to hold him for ransom. He couldn't help now but think it was his punishment for consorting with the Indian woman.

"Don' look so low, friend," said the man beside him. "As of now, yer on holiday." He laughed.

"Sure, and yer our most honored guest."

"More'n that. 'E's like one a the family."

" 'E's like a brother to me. 'Ere brother, ya'd best get started on the family chores." The man handed him his dirty plate.

"Aye. We've all got to pitch in."

They were all in agreement, and Josef was presented with a pile of tin plates.

"You can bring those out to the sea with you, friend. There's plenty of dishwater there, and you can watch yer brothers at work. Big seas last night, and we've got some harvesting to do. Lord's bounty, you know."

Josef collected the tin plates and the forks in his arms and followed the men out to the beach. To his surprise, it was only about a hundred yards off through the sea grapes. The sound of the waves had been ringing in his ears all night and morning, but he hadn't noticed it until now.

"This 'ere's Mick," said one of them. "'E's still a young lad, so 'e'll stay an 'elp ya wi' the plates. Mick's washed a lot a plates since we foun' 'im. 'E'll show ya what t'do."

"Screw the lot of ya," said Mick in his boyish voice.

"Poor Mick's an orphan. 'Is parents died in a shipwreck last year."

"Shame about that."

"If t'weren't for us, Mick'd 'ave no family 'tall."

"Poor Mick."

"'Is mother sure did die happy, though."

Mick dove after this last speaker and threw some wild, flailing punches, all of which missed the mark. The man kept smiling while he grabbed hold of Mick's wrists and held him at arm's length. Mick was red faced and puffing. He kept kicking until he finally caught him in the kneecap, and the man flinched and threw Mick to the ground. Mick couldn't quite hold back his tears.

"Don' be so sensitive, little Mick. Ya wouldn' want ta embarrass yaself in front of our guest here, would ya?"

"That's right, Mick. Now be a good little girl an' put on yer best manners for our postman."

The men left Mick and Josef behind, splitting up and walking down the shore in opposite directions as they scanned the sand and the waves for salvage. Josef was glad to be away from them for the moment. Their violence and cruelty to young

Mick was appalling and did not bode well for Josef's chances of surviving this experience intact. The U.S. Government would never believe it had hired a mail carrier so stupid as to allow himself to be kidnapped by scavenging pirates. They'd laugh at the scavengers' demands if they listened to them at all, and Josef knew he had little hope of ever being rescued or ransomed.

The day was hot and bright, and the powerful waves crashed thunderously onto the beach. One at a time, Josef took a plate and rinsed it in the foamy surf. He refused to abandon his mail sack, which made things more difficult. He had to be careful not to let the sack droop into the waves; he already had soaked it once.

"That's right," said Mick, standing over him now. "Scrub them plates."

Josef looked up at Mick and thought with pity about how young he was, probably no older than his middle teens. His hair was light, nearly blond, and his pink complexion was soft and even. Josef wondered what the boy's history really was. What horrible thing had they done to his parents? He shuddered to think. And why did he remain with these men? Was it slavery? Or perhaps he'd remained here because he had nowhere else to go, no one to go to. So now he was trying his best to fit in with them. What a horrible thing to make oneself fit into a "family" such as this. Josef felt a sudden wave of compassion.

"If you like," said Josef, "you can travel with me to Biscayne. It is possible there will be other openings in the postal service."

"What makes you think you're going anywhere?" said Mick. "You ain't never leavin here if I can help it. Arr."

"Perhaps we can escape," said Josef. "I am acquainted with a postmaster who may need someone to sort mail for him. He may provide you with a home as well."

The tenseness left the boy's face for just a moment, then

just as quickly his eyes iced again and he kicked Josef between the ribs.

"Yer livin in a fairy tale, bloody fool. Now shut yer hole and scrub them plates."

Josef had dropped the plate he was scrubbing, and now he grabbed at the pain in his side. He struggled to catch his breath. The powerful surf washed up around him and tugged at his ankles and knees. The sand clawed at his raw feet.

"Bloody stupid fool," said Mick, and he made a move like he was going to kick Josef again when a shout came from down the beach.

"Booty! Booty ho!"

In a moment, the group to the north came charging down the beach to meet the others.

"Come along, mate," said one of them, grabbing Josef and yanking him to his feet. Mick followed behind, shoving Josef between the shoulder blades if he fell back even a half step.

A few hundred yards south, they met up with the other group. One of them was holding some splinters of wood.

"Ya call that booty?" said another man, pulling the wood away.

"Arr, ya bloody stillborn. This 'ere's only a taste. Take a look out ta sea."

A hundred fifty yards offshore, a large chunk of bound wood, probably from the side of a ship, bobbed in the white-lipped swells.

"She coming our way?"

"Arr. She seems stationary."

All of them stared at it for a moment. The wood and waves repeated their movements over and over.

"Who's goin out to get her?"

"Seems a healthy young lad like Mick'd want a chance ta prove himself."

"Seems so."

"Not in sech a rile, mate. Not me. Arr."

"It's Mick."

"Aye, it's got ta be Mick."

"What if she's only the wood?" protested Mick. "I don't see no other booty. It ain't worth it, I say."

"I say it is. Even if she's only wood, she's a good hunk of it. Save us lots of carpentry, she will."

"What we need wi' more carpentry?"

"Well, we'll be needin a temporary home for our guest. We wouldn't want him to sleep in a flimsy little tent every night, would we now? Wouldn't be showin proper respect for property of the U.S. Gov'ment."

"Aye, it's the Christian thing ta do."

"Then let *him* fetch it," said Mick.

Some of them laughed. "The lad's wiser'n we give 'im credit fer."

"Aye. What say you, Mister Postman?"

Josef felt their stares and couldn't squeeze a word out of his throat.

Young Mick stepped up and got in his face. "What say you, Yank? How 'bout a little swim-and-fetch, eh?"

Josef opened his lips but couldn't speak right away. He was shaking. When he finally did speak, seemingly against his will and for the very first time in his life, he knowingly told a lie.

"I can't swim," he said.

Mick bore down on him, his pale eyes almost bursting from their sockets. "Yer lyin."

Josef immediately felt the enormous injustice he'd done to the memory of Uncle Mordy. What now of those fond memories of learning to swim? What now of the pride he'd felt at pleasing his uncle with those early successes? With a word, he'd tainted everything with the filth of disavowal.

Now he was trapped in it against all doubters and his own sense of guilt. He had to keep his eyes on Mick's face. He knew that. If he looked away he'd be caught and treated harshly— tortured to the brink of death—he'd read of the cruelties these types could inflict, solely for their own pleasure. He'd lied, and now, against everything he knew was right, he had to act as though he meant it. He felt his world had diverged into two complex and incompatible paths. There was the world he'd always known—the world of truth, the world whose path he'd faithfully sought and followed throughout his young life. And then, with this lie, he'd entered into a new world, the world of lies, where the truth held no weight; the only important thing was a person's ability to act as though he spoke truthfully. To others, the difference was irrelevant; if he acted as though he was in the world of truth, how could they ever know otherwise? But they couldn't know that the two worlds now existed simultaneously in Josef's mind. They couldn't know the pain he felt at this dark and secret world he'd unleashed from within. They couldn't see the great empty chasm that neatly divided the two worlds that, when crossed, produced the most painful feelings of guilt and shame Josef had ever known.

He shook his head, keeping his eyes on Mick. "I've never been in over my knees," he said.

"Liar!" Mick's face turned red and he drew back his fist.

Another one grabbed Mick's arm. "Leave 'im, Mick. 'E's no good to us drowned. You do it."

"I won't!"

Now the other men circled around Mick.

"Arr. You'll do it, Mick. You've no choice."

"I won't do it! The little bastard Yank's lyin. 'E's lyin, can't ya see it!"

Josef saw Mick's face between the brawny shoulders of the men. Mick suddenly looked scared and younger, almost girlish.

One of the men slapped Mick's cheek and the color went out of it. "Shut up an swim, ya stupid orphan brat or you'll end up like yer mummy and daddy!"

Several hands gave Mick a shove toward the ocean. He looked back at them once, then spit at Josef's feet.

"Ya'd best not be lyin," said a voice in Josef's ear.

Mick waded in up to his waist. The waves broke across his

chest, causing him to stumble back. Then he dove in and came up on the other side of the break, already out of breath. He started swimming, not gracefully, but with some confidence. He disappeared for seconds at a time as the waves rolled over his head. The wind had picked up and threw a spray back off the crest of the waves. Mick was nearly lost in the turbulence and mist.

"'E's not sech a bad swimmer," said one man.

"Na, he'll make it yet."

As Mick approached the wreckage, he began to disappear for longer periods of time, up to ten seconds. His swimming became more uneven as it took more effort to stay afloat. The waves dwarfed him out there, as if he were little more than a clump of seaweed. When he finally reached the wood, it seemed to be breaking up into two sections, each at least twice as big as Mick. He turned around at the last moment before he got there, as if to yell something. A victory yell, maybe, or some sort of curse he'd never say to their faces. Or maybe, Josef hoped, it was just to tell them he was okay. But if he did actually get any words out, they were lost in the ocean's roar, and the very next moment he was struck from behind when a monstrous wave slammed one section of wood into the back of his head and knocked him below the surface.

On shore, no one spoke for a moment, expecting him to come back up and wave again.

"Mick," said one of them. "Little Mick."

They waited a minute longer and Mick's head did not reappear. Someone finally spoke up.

"Who'll go out for Mick?"

Right away, a hand grasped Josef's shoulder. "'Ere's the man ought to do it. It's *his* skin Mick saved."

"Aye. Look at 'im. There ain't a ounce of grief in 'is face, and Mick volunteerin out of the goodness of 'is heart."

"What about our government ransom?"

"That money belongs with Mick, now."

"Aye."

"But I can't swim," said Josef, still trying to play by the rules of his lie.

"Way I see it, yer hide ain't worth the sand between yer toes, seein as how the man who saved yer life is out ta sea drownin as we speak."

"Sure, and 'is only chance to make good is to bring in poor Mick."

"Or what's left of 'im."

"Arr, who'd've thought we'd miss 'im?"

"Like family, 'e was."

Another hand slapped Josef on the back, blowing all the air out of him.

"It's time you learn to swim, mate."

The other men agreed, and they shoved Josef forcefully toward the water, where he fell face first into the surf. He looked back at them just in time to catch a clump of sand in his face.

"Get to it!" said one man, coming to him and kicking him into deeper water. "Mick's waitin fer ya."

Josef dragged himself in, and when he got past the break, he began to dog-paddle. He tried to look as though he were struggling, because he was still an easy pistol shot. Before he was out of earshot, though, he heard them shouting.

"You bloody liar!"

"'E swims like a fish!"

"The lyin bastard!"

Then he heard the pistols and the "thunk" of the bullets breaking the water around him. He swam as fast as he could, using the Australian crawl Uncle Mordy had taught him in the Hudson River. Yet every stroke filled him with guilt; he'd denied the beautiful memories of those swimming lessons, but still used the skills to save his cowardly hide.

The pistols kept firing, and Josef felt he had no strength at all in his arms and legs, but somehow, with the stamina of fear, he moved forward, every few seconds diving beneath the thick green whitecaps that twisted his body to rags and soaked his postal bag and all the mail in it. Somewhere between the shore and the wreckage, he understood that his entire life had amounted to nothing but failure, and now he'd failed morally as well. He felt his life was worthless, and that by all rights he deserved to die here and now. Still, something kept him going, perhaps only fear, but maybe it was the hope that he could one day redeem himself, if only in some small way.

At last the guns stopped sounding. He reached the wreckage and between waves seized hold of the ship's siding. There was no sign of Mick. The piece Josef had grabbed made a rectangular, arched raft with splintery edges. After several attempts, he pulled himself up and lay flat, clinging to the sides as the waves washed over him. When he caught his breath he heard something thumping hollowly against the underside of the wood, directly below him. He stiffened at the thought of what it might be, and then, a few waves later, his fear was confirmed. The pate of Mick's head bobbed in front of Josef's face, Mick's light hair splayed out in the water like the arms of a jellyfish, his face almost lost in the green shadows. When the next wave struck, the face turned upward for just an instant. It looked completely different now, in death. All the tenseness and the hardness that had been forced upon it had fallen away. Its features had softened so much that it hardly looked like the same person. A thought struck Josef all at once that was difficult to accept, but seemed to make perfect sense at the same time. That face he'd been looking at had not been the face of a young boy at all. For whatever reason, probably out of a desperate fear, Mick had only posed as one. He'd lived a lie since he'd been shipwrecked and captured, and that's why he'd known all along that Josef was lying about his swimming ability. Mick had seen the diverging worlds forming in Josef's mind, and knew what a person had to do sometimes to save his skin. Mick had understood that sometimes living a lie was the only alternative when you wanted nothing more than to live. Because Mick had done it herself.

Chapter 12

WHEN JOSEF LIFTED his head again, it was to rub salt out of his eyes. Hours must have passed. The sea had calmed and the scavengers were nowhere in sight. Still, the hollow sound of Mick's head bobbing against the raft had not rung itself out of Josef's ears.

He seemed to be drifting southward. He'd drifted out to sea a little way, too, though the shore was still in clear view. The wind had calmed, and for the first time in two days Josef felt the full brunt of the sun. His shirt had ripped, and part of his back was exposed—he could feel exactly where.

He lifted himself to a sitting position and looked nervously at the sea around him. No sign of Mick. Thinking it was safe now to head for shore, he yanked up one of the loose planks of wood and began to paddle. He propelled himself at an almost undetectable speed and filled his hands with splinters, but if he let himself drift, he might come across the Gulf Stream, and then there'd be no hope at all—he knew that from his books. In the Gulf Stream, he'd be carried north up the coast, toward the Carolinas, past Long Island and agonizingly close to his wife and aunt in Brooklyn, then up to Nova Scotia, Newfoundland, and beyond! Perhaps he'd catch other currents and then drift down along the coasts of Europe and Africa and back across the Atlantic in an endless and unbreakable circle. The current would hold him in its watery grasp, and what grief to drift eternally like that, nearly always within sight of land!

That fear alone was enough to keep him paddling. He put everything he had into it, and within an hour he saw he'd made progress. After two hours, his raft split apart in the break, and he swam the last hundred yards to shore. But the ocean currents had only been half his trouble. As he stumbled out of the surf, he was cured and marinated to perfection and ready to be roasted by the midday sun.

He looked down at his mail sack. It had hung from his neck throughout the entire ordeal and now, thoroughly soaked, it was an emblem of his incompetence. He dared not look inside it. If the letters and packages had not been shredded into pulp, they were at least unreadable.

Seeing no humans or animals to endanger him, Josef continued south along his mail route. At first he felt some contentment and relief. The simple, regular action of walking in the sand helped him to forget his recent troubles for a moment. He'd been through a lot, and it felt good to be back on the job again, though now the delivery was probably pointless.

But he was quickly reminded that walking the beach at this time of day was little consolation. His feet hadn't had time to heal. Still red and sore, they began to throb in the heat. His skin began to blister where his shirt had ripped open.

The waves had kicked up a thick mist of ocean that hadn't yet settled. This made breathing heavy and unsatisfying. He wheezed as he walked. He'd had little food since Lena left him, and he suddenly grew desperately hungry. There'd be food waiting for him at the Biscayne post office, but Biscayne seemed like a dream to him now, a faint image of his unreachable paradise.

The pain from the hot sand seemed to be the only thing keeping his feet moving. After a while, the sand grew too hot and his reactions too slow to make it bearable; he had to descend the beach and splash through the surf, so his pace slowed to a crawl.

It wasn't long before his mind began to wander, perhaps in a natural defense against the torture of the elements, or perhaps in a prelude to madness. He tried to think joyful thoughts, of happier times. Yet every thought from his past led him down a fateful path to the horror of young Mick's death, and the lying cowardice that caused it. He saw clearly how weak-willed and deceitful he truly was, and how truly unfit he was for the New Paradise he'd only recently imagined so vividly. Even that image he now saw as little more than a cowardly haven to justify his own fears and prejudices. It hadn't taken long for him to exclude the breeds of animals he didn't like, or to admit the Indians as mere slaves working the great fans so Josef alone (and maybe a few close friends and family) could be happy and comfortable in the breeze. It hadn't taken long for him to raise carnal pleasures to the one supremely important ingredient. Why, his view of paradise had become little more than a Roman bath house! A self-aggrandizing fantasy! It hadn't taken him long, either, to prove himself unworthy of even the most pale replica of Paradise. He hadn't the purity of heart, or even a morsel of human compassion. Here was the paradise he deserved—alone and aching, on a beach too hot to walk and a surf that made him deny the happiest moments of his life, where the waves washed up and poured salt into his wounds and the sting of his sweat burned tracks in his raw skin, and the hollow thunk of Mick's blonde pate cursed every step of his blistered and overexposed Brooklynite's feet.

He saw Lena now, in her flowing white wedding dress, and her great innocent smile of hope. She'd trusted him with the fulfillment of her own dreams, and he'd let her down in selfish pursuit of his private fancies. What a fool he'd been to bring her to the tropics! Any clear-thinking person could see she was not suited for it. Why did he think she'd grow accustomed to such a place? Why would she want to? She'd come only because she loved Josef, and he'd destroyed their marriage for the sake of his greed for glory. Like a fool, he thought he'd been meant for greatness. But it was clear he was an ordinary man at best, weak-willed and cowardly, deceitful and selfish, full of foolish dreams.

He saw Lena in her white dress, standing before him on the beach, always just out of reach, as though he were trapped forever in the Gulf Stream off the coast of Lena. Then her image began to waver and her features hardened and her hair shortened and changed color and suddenly there was young Mick standing before him, her foot cocked and ready to kick him for the injustice he'd done her. And he begged her, "Please kick me, please kick me, Lena. I deserve to be kicked by the one I love, painfully and forever kicked." And he got down in the wash of the waves and begged her, "Kick me!" but always as the foot began its motion toward his ribs, the image disappeared with the sound of a *thunk*.

It was a hollow *thunk*, like a book slammed shut or a fist striking a nose. Delirious, Josef attributed the sound to his own feet splashing in the surf, and he edged deeper and deeper into the water until the waves crashed across his waist, soaking the mail sack before it had fully dried out. He waded slowly, the sun's reflection blinding him, his legs driven with a dumb life of their own. He was crazed and stumbling, and his whole body burned and ached. He mumbled as he walked, "Kick me, please kick me, Lena!" But always he was let down, and he cringed at the sound only he could hear: *thunk*.

It was late afternoon when he stumbled, breathless, dehydrated, and half crazy, onto several dozen men and women grouped on the beach just up from the posh Biscayne Grand Hotel. The group was fancily dressed in whites and pastels they'd had tailored just for their trip to the tropics. The women carried parasols. They were watching a salvage operation offshore, where a ship had broken up on the reef.

Josef walked through them, perhaps a little faster now, knowing he'd almost made it. As he did so, he bumped into

some of them, and they turned and looked on him with horror—his face was red and taut, and his blackened eyes and broken nose had still not fully healed from that night in the postmaster's restaurant. He wheezed and snorted as he dragged
himself through the sunny crowd, some of whom made
comments on his appearance and odor. But after their initial
shock, they merely stepped back and let him pass, because
they were wealthy Northeasterners whose tropical holiday
had already been interrupted, though not unpleasantly, by the
excitement of the shipwreck. All of them agreed, without
having to say a word about it, that one bit of excitement could
be dandy, but two at once was probably a strain to one's constitution. And what with the ladies here and all, it would be
better just to ignore this strange creature—this medicine man,
or this crocodile breeder, or whatever he might be—and keep
one's attention focused on this interesting shipwreck, so that
each and every detail could be gathered into a fascinating tale
to relate to one's friends and colleagues back home.

Yet there was one man who stood out from this group, if
only for the darker colors of his attire and the general careless-
ness—almost slovenliness—with which he wore it. He was a
short, blank-faced gent with a thin moustache and dark, dark
eyes. His bowler was pulled down just a little too far for the
day's fashion, and that made him seem as though he had something to hide. He was a reporter on assignment for the *New
York Times* and had been sent to file a story about the growth
of the transportation and trade industries in Florida, and the
problems encountered in laying tracks and roads, and dredg-
ing channels and harbors. He was also to focus on the toll that
the inhospitable subtropical climate took on the hundreds of
northern workers who'd been brought in to do the work by big
northern holding companies seeking footholds in the un-
tapped marketplace. This shipwreck was timely and served
his story to a tee, yet something in the corner of his eye made
him stop his note-taking and look up.

He saw Josef moving in his direction, and he took a good

look at Josef's blazing red skin, the broken and discolored nose that hadn't set properly, the trickle of blood that had dried on Josef's upper lip, and the crazed and black-ringed eyes that seemed unable to focus, and the reporter thought he was looking at some evil apparition, lacking only the claws and horns to be a full-fledged voodoo devil. But he also knew he was looking at a damned good story.

"Say, bud," said the reporter.

Josef stopped at the voice and his head fell to his chest. He couldn't pull it up to look the man in the eye.

"You from the wreck out there?" asked the reporter.

"Wreck," repeated Josef, his hoarse voice barely more than a whisper.

"SS *Hudson Valley*. Captain put her into the reef last night." He laughed. "Some of the locals say he must've been mesmerized by a mermaid or a siren or something. Company doesn't buy it. He's got a history with the bottle, you know. Local sheriff's holding 'im while they investigate. Say, you look like you've been through hell. You don't know nothing about it?"

Josef turned the weathered and damp mail sack in front of him to identify himself as a carrier. It hurt too much to speak.

"Ah," said the reporter, "you from that town north of here? What's it called?—Figulus?"

Josef lifted his head a fraction of an inch to nod.

"I heard they got plans for a shipping terminal up there—any truth to that?"

Josef coughed the sweat away from his lips, and the reporter took this as a negative.

"Well hey, bud," said the reporter. "I'm John Thomas. *New York Times*. Thanks for the info."

He held his hand out, but Josef couldn't raise his more than twenty degrees, so John Thomas was forced to stretch his reach. He was shocked at the heat he felt coming from that hand. It was as though it had an energy source all its own.

Then Josef started forward again, remembering he was

nearly there. The reporter followed him with his eyes, and noticed for the first time and with great surprise Josef's burned and uncovered feet. They were astonishingly weather-beaten, and it was amazing they could still be of any use at all to their owner.

When Josef turned inland, toward the post office, John Thomas turned his attention back to the wreck. But he found it difficult to concentrate on his story. The encounter with Josef had started his mind whirring. *There is something to this man,* he thought. It was something he could not as yet define, but something that had begun, in fits and flashes, to take shape in his reporter's brain.

THE BISCAYNE POSTMASTER, Elijah J. Partridge, read what he could of the note from Postmaster Shank and gave Josef a surly welcome: Josef was a day late; he had let the postal sack drag in the water, and few of the letters and packages would ever reach their destination now—the addresses had been washed away by the surf, and some of the letters were nothing but tattered rags; this was an outrage in the eyes of the U.S. Government, a disservice to the entire country; furthermore, what had he done with his government-issued postal shoes?—only a fool would lose the shoes off his feet and expose that sensitive skin; those shoes had been expressly designed, and at great cost to the nation at large, to protect the carrier's feet from the elements—snow, sleet, rain, hail, what have you—that fool postmaster in Figulus must have left his wits at home when he hired such an imbecile for so important a position!

Partridge continued to mutter indignantly as he filled Josef's sack with northbound mail. Josef hadn't the energy to put forth a word in his defense. He could only think with horror about the awful journey back to Figulus. Defeat whispered loudly in his ear, though he couldn't collect his wits enough to understand it.

"Now these letters on top here have to be dropped off at the port on your way out," said Partridge. "We have important guests at the hotels and they have to keep in touch with their families and business associates."

Josef nodded.

"Now be on your way and for God's sake get some coverings for your feet." Partridge returned to mail-sorting, shaking his head.

At last Josef dragged himself out of the office and returned to the sunlight.

Still unsure of what he was going to do or where he might go, with growing doubts about who he was, even, Josef walked back toward the beach, moving his feet without the will to do so. He'd already forgotten about his delivery to the port.

His first step onto the sand seemed to wake him out of his trance, and he understood fully the extent of his failure. He had failed his wife first of all by dragging her into the nightmare of pioneer life. But that might have been rectified were it not for his carnal frolic with that squaw. He'd been with the squaw before he'd even consummated his marriage, and what kind of man did that?! He'd failed his fellow settlers in Figulus by destroying their letters to family, friends, and loved ones, letters posted in the solemn and unspoken trust that exists between a community and its postal carrier. He'd failed his dear uncle by not locating the fine loafers he'd practically sent from his death bed, and by failing to have the courage and strength of will to conquer the inconveniences of the tropics, and worst of all by denying the love and kindness his uncle had shown in teaching Josef to swim. Then there was his grandest failure of all: he'd failed his vision of Paradise and thus failed God Himself, for what is a man if he can't do the work of the Lord? He'd been sent a beautiful image of the Paradise to come, and he'd been handed a role in its creation, but he'd taken it upon himself to revise the Lord's will. There'd been handwriting on the wall, and he'd taken the liberty to edit it for his own selfish whims. He'd proved in the eyes of both God and man that he was nothing more than a fool, a nobody destined for an unremarkable life among all the other nobodies and their visions of personal contentment.

Such was Josef's state as he stepped into the quiet Atlantic, mellow with late-afternoon sunlight. He stared at the horizon and was suddenly overwhelmed by a great sense of relief. It was an odd and seemingly inappropriate feeling, so much so that it made him weightless and giddy. He'd recognized himself for an incompetent fool, and as sad as the thought was at first, it now reemerged with a secondary effect: in acknowledging his failure, he had in one fell swoop relieved himself of all obligations to everyone and everything—all the weight of conquering the wilderness, of living up to the memory of his uncle, and of serving the Will of the Lord had been lifted from his shoulders. He trembled at this airy gift of freedom. He felt he could step up and walk on these waves, all the way to Africa if he so desired. He was giddy with foolishness. What a happy, stupid fool he was!

So he couldn't help but break out in laughter, and he laughed like never before, loudly and without restraint, for he was now the town fool, of whom nothing was expected and nothing demanded. He was a joker in the deck, the wild card used by anyone for any purpose, and it was nothing to him because he himself was nothing. He laughed so loudly and with such abandon that he seemed to put something of himself in that laugh, and he sent it out across the quiet ocean like a message in a new tongue, a tongue so ambiguous that anyone receiving the message, no matter which language he spoke, would be free to read it in any way he so desired and use it for any purpose he so wished. It was laughter rich and resounding, a thing of pure and absolute beauty, the purest and truest thing Josef had ever made.

Then he cut it off all at once and lifted his mail sack off his neck and shoulder and raised it above his head, and with a shot-putter's shout and a determination greater than any he'd known in his young life, he heaved the mail sack far out into the glassy water, where it disappeared with a ripple beneath a floating bed of seaweed.

Finally, in the first hints of darkness, he made his way to the docks at the Port of Biscayne, and up the ramp to the lone steamer anchored there. He spoke to the bursar who was ready to close up for the night until Josef asked to book passage. The man began to complete the forms for a ticket until he learned Josef's name and he put his pen down and opened up a little drawer in his desk.

"Your wife was on our line just last week, sir," he said. "She already booked your passage."

The color went out of Josef's face. He took the ticket and smiled faintly. She'd known all along. She knew him better than he knew himself. He went up on deck and located the first-class cabin Lena had reserved for him, inserted the key, closed the door behind him, and collapsed on the oversized bed in complete exhaustion and utter contentment.

PART III

The Legend of the Barefoot Mailman

Chapter 13

Having spent the last of his expense account at the Biscayne Grand Hotel's lavish bar, John Thomas boarded the same steamer for New York as Josef Steinmetz. He had plenty of firsthand information to write his assigned story for the *Times*, but as he'd sipped his eighth gin and tonic the night before, he'd come to a certain conclusion about what to do with his pages and pages of notes on the Florida transportation industry and the progress it had made toward linking the last of the Eastern wilds with the rest of the United States.

John Thomas was sick of his grind as a *Times* reporter. Though he was just thirty years old, he'd risen to be one of the star traveling reporters for the newspaper. He was being groomed for a high editorial position. Still, it was unsatisfying for him. He knew he was a brilliant writer. He'd read the work of all the great reporters of his day and could identify their styles even without their bylines. In terms of sheer reporting, he was on a par with the best of them. He'd said as much to his editor and his fellow reporters, because John Thomas was an ambitious man and not prone to attacks of self-effacement. Secretly, though, he knew he was better. What prevented him from saying that much was the inkling of modesty he could display when it was prudent. His writing, as he saw it, was qualitatively different from the other great reporters of his day. He had a certain flair for finding the story where others failed. He had more than just the power of the pen; he had that rare and delicate touch that could transform the mundane, insignificant events of this world into the most wondrous of dramas. *And that is the mark of the great ones*, he thought. *To see what the others do not, and by the genius of my pen, to convey the secrets of the world. I'm a guide, a prophet, and—who's to argue?—a creator.*

Operating with this knowledge, it was difficult for him to put up with deadlines, fussy editors, and jealous colleagues. He'd paid his dues for ten years and enough was enough. He had the talent and the confidence to make his run to the top, and now he saw an opportunity to use the *Times* the way he'd always thought it *should* be used—as a stepping stone to greatness.

John Thomas boarded the steamer that morning and took the cabin paid for by his paper, a nice cabin, but not first class. When the ship left port and sailed through the inlet and out into the open sea, when it had settled into a comfortable rumble northward, he went up on deck with his pages and pages of notes and tore them one by one out of his notebook, letting them fly into the warm, green waters of the Gulf Stream.

Although they were passengers together on that same ship, Josef Steinmetz and John Thomas never met during the voyage. The ship's doctor treated Josef for overexposure and ordered him to remain in bed for the duration of the voyage and perhaps for weeks longer—so he reclined by himself in his first-class cabin. But there was little chance of him leaving there anyway—his feet were beyond hope; the doctor could only shake his head in pity, rub the feet with aloe, prop them up with pillows, and order Josef to keep them out of the light.

John Thomas also closed himself in his cabin after he let fly his notes, but for different reasons. He pushed himself with his writing, working more intensely than ever before. Rather than a dry, factual story suitable for the business pages, he

would write a dramatic piece with a theme of the perseverance and triumph of the human spirit. This would be his ca-
reer piece, his ticket to the Ball of the Immortals.

He worked long hours to complete this piece before the
ship docked in New York. Once there, he collected his papers
—he'd revised the story four times, keeping the drafts for the
future scholars of his work—and made his way straight to
Times Square and the offices of the *New York Times*.

He marched into the office of Nile Lesterton, his editor,
and was greeted warmly with a cigar and a slap on the back.
Lesterton thought of Thomas as his star pupil, and took no
small credit for Thomas's accomplishments. Thomas had detected this attitude long ago, and it made him laugh inwardly,
though on one level he found it a refreshing change from the
professional jealousy of his other colleagues.

Thomas brushed aside Lesterton's questions about the
Florida transportation business and moved right into his pitch
for the story he'd worked up on the boat. He gave it his all,
knowing he had nothing to fall back on, that the notes for his
assignment were at that very moment drifting in the Gulf
Stream, dissolving in the action of the waves and the nibbles
of fish and the natural entropy of things left unattended.

Of course the editor was taken aback at first, criticizing
the piece for its "literariness." But the reporter delivered the
eloquent and inspired speech he'd also written and rehearsed
on the ship, touching on the value of human-interest stories
and the importance of legends as a binding influence on this
vast and sometimes fractured nation of ours—legends as the
roux in the great melting pot—and in the end, the editor con-
sented to print it.

The story was published in five parts, made an immediate
sensation in New York, and was soon reprinted in some of the
major newspapers throughout the Northeast. It outlined the
true and sensational tale of a man known only as "The Barefoot Mailman," who, as a boy, had been shipwrecked in Florida
and raised by Seminole Indians. When he reached puberty, he

wasn't allowed to enter the rites of passage and become a brave, but was sent off to rejoin his own people. He fell in with a group of settlers in the town of Figulus who ostracized him because of his mysterious background and his familiarity with the heathens. But once the town of Figulus was incorporated, they found a use for him—he had a native's knowledge of the land, something valuable, possibly life-saving, on the long, arduous routes of Florida postal carriers. So they took a chance and hired him to deliver and retrieve their mail from the post office in Biscayne, a full sixty miles to the south. Proud to serve his country, he made the strenuous journey up and down the Florida coast, delivering the mail under the harshest of conditions, and all in his bare feet, for, despite his ease in re-learning the language and customs of the white man, he kept the memory of his Seminole upbringing alive by retaining this single Indian custom. It was in the white man's honor that he served his country so, and it was in the red man's honor that he did it in his bare feet.

The story was punctuated with words from the Mailman himself, whom John Thomas claimed to have followed and interviewed at length, braving the forbidding jungles and the violent weather until a tropical fever finally forced the reporter to cooler climes, leaving the Mailman to continue his brave and solitary duties.

The Barefoot Mailman became an instant legend, striking a chord with the public's thirst for adventure and for positive, hard-working role models. For the down-and-out he became a symbol of perseverance. For new immigrants, he became a symbol of the American Dream, of finding a niche in a strange new world. The legend made its way into several children's books, and kids listened, wide-eyed and drooling, as their mamas read them the great adventure tale from the picture books—they were enraptured by the mystery of the strange land while they were provided with a model of courage and strength. A popular song made the rounds in those days, too:

Barefoot Man

Oh barefoot man, oh barefoot man,
post me a note with your tom-tom band.
Make it to my uncle, in Kalamazoo,
make it to my aunt, in Katmandu.
Tell 'em that I love 'em, and tell 'em I'm blessed.
Knock it out in tom-tom, and send 'em my best.

Oh barefoot man, oh barefoot man,
send me up a signal to my best girl, Nan.
Address it to Milwaukee, Route Number Two,
the little pink house where the love-birds roost.
Ain't no need for walkin', just send it with smoke,
so cover up your feet and let my love note float.

Finally, as if the legend needed further acknowledgment to
solidify its influence, it was alluded to in numerous literary
works of the period as a symbol of the evolutionary adaptability of man.

For John Thomas, it was all a confirmation of what he already knew about his talents and the lifelong feeling he'd had
that he'd been destined for greatness. At the first hint of the
legend's creating a stir, he quit his job at the *Times* and began
to put together a book on the subject. The quick popularity of
the legend had made him anxious—people were capitalizing
on his baby. But a book would secure his position as minister
of the legend and once and for all eternity bind his name together with the Legend of the Barefoot Mailman.

PART IV

The Legend of Josef Steinmetz

Chapter 14

EARL SHANK WAITED twenty-two days for his mail carrier to bring the mail up from Biscayne. After nine days, he'd thought he noticed the first stirrings of anxiety in Mely's face. She didn't say anything, but the silence was loaded. At first, they avoided the issue by avoiding any reference to the mail. Gradually, though, the gaps in their daily banter grew like a hole in a sock that eventually makes it more hole than sock. They avoided references to the post office, to the restaurant, to grapefruits and oranges, to Yankees, and to foreigners, so that by the morning of the twenty-second day, they woke up with almost nothing they could say to each other. Earl thought how odd it was that the little man had worked himself into their thoughts so thoroughly in such a short time. They barely knew the man, and yet they acted like the parents of a child lost at sea.

As they sat at the table trying to choke down their grapefruit and avoid each other's eyes, Mely finally broke the silence.

"Earl, folks'll be expecting their mail soon. And Martha Oglesby's got a birthday package she wants to get to her mother in Savannah."

"I know, Mely. She's been tellin ever'one in town at the top of her blasted voice."

"It's time to face up to it."

Earl chewed on his lip and sighed. "The chain's been broke," he said, knowing that this had far greater implications than the delivery of Martha Oglesby's package of hand-carved coconut-husk figurines. He had clung to that little foreigner like his last hope. Now everything seemed lost—the events of his life had lost their divine, up-reaching structure and crumbled into random and microscopic insignificance. The denouement had proved nothing but a cheap shot, the playwright a cruel and undertalented jokester.

"I took the shoes out of the box," said Earl. "I durn near put 'em on his feet. He jes wouldn't have nothin to do with 'em."

"You're being silly, Earl."

"He wouldn't take the job wearin shoes. I had pressure comin down on me all the way from Washington. My name was about to be logged into the problem folder on the President's desk."

"It ain't yer fault, Earl."

"You don't understand the pressures of a government job, Mely. I got the weight of a nation on my shoulders. When the chain breaks, the whole system collapses. Commerce grinds to a halt. Hearts get broke. Friends turn against one another. The rule of law is overthrown. The president gets out of touch. National security is endangered—"

Mely slapped him across the face. "Ya can't take responsibility for the entire world, Earl. I know ya'd like to, but ya can't, because yer nothin but a reg'lar fella. Maybe ya got a bigger heart than most and that's why I put up with ya, but yer also a bigger fool than most, and yer gettin older and foolisher by the minute."

Earl sighed, rubbing his cheek, knowing she was all wrong. But it was okay, because he knew that, if nothing else, he was living for the chance to prove it to her.

"Now I ain't gone ta mention what you oughtta and oughtn't ta done with that poor man," said Mely, "and the world ain't gone ta collapse if the mail's a few days late. But

146

ya'd better get busy and find that carrier or get us a new one soon or Martha Oglesby's liable to collapse yer head in with one of her coconuts."

Earl kissed her hand and got up from the table.

"Where you going?"

"I reckon I'm headed down the beach."

"Don't be ridiculous, Earl. You wouldn't make it two miles afore you died of exhaustion."

"When I was doin publicity, I use ta make the trip ta Biscayne once a week."

"That was more'n twenty years ago, Earl, 'fore you had a pot belly the size of Lake Okeechobee. Now set down an finish yer breakfast."

"But I got ta do something, Mely. I can't help feelin guilty about that Steinmetz feller."

"If ya got to go down there, at least let Josh McCready paddle ya in his boat."

Earl came over and hugged Mely in her chair, covering her ear and neck with dry little kisses. "Yer a wise, wise woman, Mely, and I love ya for it."

And then he sat down and finished his grapefruit.

AFTER BREAKFAST, EARL stopped by Josh McCready's house and asked when he was making his next trip down to Biscayne. Josh was a retired sea captain, ten years older than Earl, but with twice his strength and five times his stamina. Josh fished now, mostly for himself, but every now and then he had a few good days in a row, and then, weather and seas permitting, he took a boatload of snapper and dolphin down to Biscayne, where he'd sell it to the Biscayne Grand Hotel or one of the other fancy resorts on the beach. "Just to keep myself busy," Josh would say. And it just so happened that although he had only a few fish to sell in the market, Josh was looking for something to keep himself busy, so he offered to leave for Biscayne. Earl changed his mind about going along. He'd ridden in Josh's boat before and knew that Josh refused to play the role of anything but captain in his own boat, and thus refused to do any rowing if there was a first mate handy to do it for him.

Earl told Josh to look for signs of the missing carrier along the beach and then to check in with Postmaster Partridge down in Biscayne. "If he ain't been seen in Biscayne in the past few days, we'd best hire a new man," Earl said gravely. And then he got an idea that gave him some hope. Remembering what he could of Josef's résumé, he dashed off an ad for a new carrier, thinking that if he could get someone with Josef's qualifications and demeanor, that someone might still deliver Earl his fortune. He knew there was no one left in Figulus who met that description, so he gave the note to Josh and told him to hang it in the Biscayne Post Office.

—◆—

WANTED FOR HIRE

By the Postal Service of the United States of America,

A Strong, Honest Man

Who Holds No Grudges
And Does Not Get Seasick on Small Boats,
For the Position of

MAIL CARRIER

on the
Figulus to Biscayne "Beach Route"
with primary obligation to

THE BEAUTIFUL, BOUNTEOUS

TOWN OF FIGULUS.

Apply in person to
EARL K. SHANK, POSTMASTER,
Town of Figulus,
OR TO MR. JOSH MCCREADY WHILE HE IS HERE ON BUSINESS.

—◆—

THE MAN WHO took the job, whom McCready brought back with him, was also a retired seafarer, Silas Lautermilch. Earl had his doubts when he saw him. He looked and acted nothing like Josef—he talked too much, and he was short and old, with thick, stumpy legs. This man looked even less able than Josef to hold up against the elements. He could walk all right, but his gait was bowlegged and his steps were about half the length of a normal man's. Thus, Earl calculated, it would take him nearly twice as long as a normal man to walk the route.

But the new carrier had no intention of walking. He'd brought his own skiff with him, and since he was familiar with the waterways and offshore currents up and down the east coast of Florida, he was going to row and sail his way to Biscayne and back.

Earl had thought of this before, but had never found anyone with a sailor's knowledge willing to take the job of mail carrier. *This is progress*, he thought, which he generally approved of, but which made him anxious now. It reminded him how quickly the state was growing. He'd already heard of a man named Flagler who meant to run a railroad line from Jacksonville all the way to Key West. That would change things faster than he could keep up with. As for this new carrier, he'd be obsolete before he knew what hit him; he'd be transferred down to Biscayne or up to St. Augustine and forced to deliver door to door, like a traveling salesman or a confidence man. But there was another aspect of progress Earl could not even imagine: John Thomas, the *New York Times* reporter, was at that moment making a legend out of a situation that had already ceased to exist.

Earl felt no nostalgia, since it had never occurred to him that the beach route was anything but painful drudgery. He didn't have the genius of a John Thomas; he had only his ambitions and the purity of his mediocrity. But he did feel anxiety, because he knew there wasn't much time left before his dreams of success would be pilfered completely by the millionaire carpetbaggers who knew potential when they saw it and had the money and the power to take advantage of it.

For the first time in his life, Earl felt old. He figured his last opportunity to make good had disappeared with Josef Steinmetz. He saw it all now as a stupid pipe dream, carried with him all these years only because of his childhood failures, a dream he'd clung to so foolishly and desperately that he'd let his last hopes rest on a scrawny little Yankee immigrant. He'd become so single-minded that he was willing to send an innocent man out to walk the beach in his bare feet, knowing full well the consequences but denying them with his selfishness. Well now there'd be no more self-deception; he'd sent a man to his death. Earl K. Shank was a murderer.

"Quit indulging in self-pity," said Mely, finally fed up after Earl had moped around the house muttering for a week straight. "You flatter yerself when ya say ya killed a man. I see the workins of that yarn spinner that rolls between yer fat ears. Yer makin yerself a story ta tell yer cronies when yer settin around playin cards and drinkin whiskey ten years from now. So nip it in the bud, Earl. Ya ain't killed a man, and ya ain't got no business makin up stories that ya did."

"But I did, Mely, and there ain't no denyin it."

"Ya done no such thing. Ya ain't killed him any more'n the mail sack ya gave 'im. Ya ain't killed 'im any more'n the President of the United States killed 'im. So stop yer mopin and go 'bout yer business again. Ya ain't been in the restaurant in weeks now. It's liable to crumble if ya don't keep it patched up."

"Let it crumble."

"You big baby. It ain't filled with ghosts, Earl."

"Yes it is, Mely. The ghosts of all my ruined dreams. The ghosts of my dark, murderer's soul."

"Stop it, Earl. If you ain't going in there, I'll go m'self. I'm thinking maybe I'll open her up tomorrow, invite folks in fer some of that leftover boar we bought off Nathan. Lord knows we need somethin to cut the gloom around here."

Earl could only hang his head and stare at his shoes, amazed at how a few thin strips of leather could separate an honest man from a murderer.

Mely walked next door to the restaurant and pried open the door that Earl had nailed shut.

If Earl had been in a better state of mind, he'd have seen the good omen in this. Maybe it was a change of heart or maybe just a gift, but Mely had taken the smallest of steps toward his way of seeing things. She was opening the restaurant and giving away free food. What better publicity than that?

THE NEXT DAY, Silas Lautermilch returned from Biscayne after his first mail run. Everything had gone fine, and he'd made the journey in record time, even though, he admitted, he'd stayed an extra day in Biscayne to drink with some old friends there.

Besides the regular mail, he handed over a package addressed to "Postmaster, Town of Figulus." Earl weighed it in his hands and trembled in fear of the worst; the package seemed just the right size and weight to contain a gruesome expression of Josef's fate. What a perfect item to hang around the neck of a fool who had gone too far.

Fingers shaking, he loaded up Silas with the southbound mail and sent him off without more than a few words. It took ten minutes for his curiosity to overcome his fear, but it did at last, and Earl sliced open the package, trying to avoid touching it too much, expecting something thick and red to ooze out onto the counter. Instead, he found another package inside with a letter attached:

Dear Postmaster:
    Enclosed please find a package recovered from the wreckage of the SS *Hudson Valley*, of which I had, until recently, been captain.
    Let me explain. At the hour of dusk on September 7, I spotted something bobbing in the waves about fifteen degrees

off our starboard bow. I directed the helmsman to steer her in for a closer look.

In hindsight, this was an unwise maneuver. My mate caught this box up in a net, but we'd steered her in too close. Before I had so much as weighed the package in my hands, my ship ran aground on the reef off Biscayne. This you have certainly read of in newspaper accounts. Let me tell you that the reports of mesmerizing mermaids are false. I may have uttered some such nonsense in my grievous delirium, and when the press got wind of it, they locked onto it and embellished it with all their imaginative powers (despite my subsequent letters to the editor).

Here, then, is the package, which I have instructed the local sheriff to forward to you, as "Figulus" is the only portion of the address still legible. It has not been opened or tampered with, damaged only by the natural force of the sea. I hope you can find its rightful owner.

Sincerely,
Capt. Melman Scrotch
Inmate, Biscayne City Jail

Even before he sliced open the inside box and pulled out the loafers, Earl knew that fate had once again smiled upon him. He was a fool indeed—a fool to ever doubt that good fortune would find its way back to him even if that young immigrant didn't. Because it was *his* good fortune—*of course*—and that little foreigner had been only its carrier; he'd brought Earl's fortune here from God-knows-where, and he'd tried his best to run away with it again. But if nothing else was yet clear to Earl, this one fact was: that when a man's fortune discovers the whereabouts of its rightful owner, it will always find its way home, no matter who takes it and how far astray it is taken. And later, when the implications of this event and the discovery of its hidden meaning became fully known to him, Earl would know that in the autobiography of Earl Shank, this one shining moment, this single and never-to-be-repeated gesture of slicing open the box and pulling out a pair of loafers, would warrant an entire chapter.

It was a single, fluid, and intensely meaningful motion that produced the shoes for him—a gesture of religious significance, a high priest reaching into the sacrificial lamb and pulling forth the still-beating heart. There they were, cherry brown, made of the finest imported leather, supple and alive to the touch. A film of dried seawater coated the shoes inside and out, and Earl instinctively went to work with a cloth, rubbing and buffing and blowing off the dust, and thinking, *This is a sign of forgiveness, and it's tellin me somethin like, "Earl, ya ain't no murderer after all, yer jest a man doin his job and tryin ta work through his destiny, and sometimes the path ta that destiny crosses through some dang'res territory, but there's always some high ground jest ahead, and a pair a shoes ta get ya there."*

And even if he ain't dead, thought Earl, slipping into the shoes, *there ain't no way of findin where he is. And seein, then, that these here shoes ain't got a rightful owner, I reckon I'm the next best thing.*

They were narrow in the toes, and there was no way he was going to get his heels in there, but they were still the finest shoes he had ever worn. The finest he'd ever seen, even. When he wore these shoes he could feel their soft glow as if the moon itself was begging at his feet. He felt, too, the stirring of the old fire, as if now he could hope against all hope that his dreams would not be crushed in the end.

Chapter 15

CAPTAIN MELMAN SCROTCH had lied in his letter to the postmaster of Figulus. He was not the one who'd given the order to move in and retrieve the package of shoes. In fact, he'd strongly advised against it, given the rough seas and the ship's proximity to the reef. But a ship's captain is not truly the master of his ship when the ship's owner is aboard, and Captain Scrotch had had the dubious honor of playing host to Mr. Elias Rathmartin, millionaire adventurer and owner of Southwind Cruise Lines and Shipping and Trading Company, New York, New York.

If anyone had made good the promise of the American Dream, it was Elias Rathmartin. He was a poor orphan who'd climbed his way up the great ladder, and he hadn't stepped on all that many hands in the process. In past years, Mr. Rathmartin had liked to boast that his company had more ships in its fleet than the United States Navy. He was proud of Southwind; he'd built it from the ground up. He was proud of himself, too. But there came a time, at sixty-eight years old, when his business stopped being the most important thing in his life, and he at last began to break his inveterate work habits and live just as he'd always wanted to.

Over the last two years, he'd slowly relieved himself of responsibilities to his company, leaving the day-to-day operations to his sons, Merwyn and Stanislaw. Then he took to the sea. It was a funny thing for a shipping magnate, but he'd never once stepped foot in the ocean. As a youth, he'd devoured the high-seas adventure tales that had been donated to his orphanage. The whaling adventures, the conquests of new lands, the shipwreck tales, the tales of bare-breasted island women and nose-ringed cannibals—all of these had filled his youthful fantasies and led him, when he was just nineteen, to seek investors for the purchase of a well-worn trading ship. Still, though he continued to read the adventure tales throughout his adult life, he'd never once ventured out of his home port, on vacation or business or otherwise. He was too caught up in the day-to-day operation in his New York offices, too driven to tear himself away.

So it wasn't until he was seventy years old that Elias Rathmartin even stood on one of his ships while it was docked in the harbor. Only then did he set off in search of the great adventure he'd always read about. But no one had ever dared to tell Elias Rathmartin that mermaids and sea monsters weren't real, or that lost cities of gold didn't sometimes reappear from the depths. Respectful acquaintances and Southwind employees might call him eccentric; another possibility occurred to those who knew him best.

One ship in the company's fleet was commissioned for his personal use, for netting mermaids and tempting the monsters of the Sargasso Sea. This was distressing to his tight-fisted sons, who wanted nothing more than to keep careful account of their much-deserved inheritance. But they dared not say anything to his face.

It was on one of these adventures that Rathmartin had ordered Captain Scrotch in for a closer look at what he suspected was a foundering mermaid. The results of this maneuver landed Rathmartin in the hospital in Biscayne, and landed Captain Scrotch in jail. Scrotch had only obeyed orders, but he was a company man, and he took the fall to save his boss the embarrassment, knowing he'd be restored to captain after a few unpaid weeks in jail.

The experience of the shipwreck, although every bit as perilous and exciting as he'd always hoped, turned out to be a bit much for Elias Rathmartin. Though he'd never once touched the water—the ship's mate had lifted him into the lifeboat and lifted him out again when they reached the shore—his personal physician had detected a slight murmur of the heart and thought it best that Elias rest up for a few weeks in the local hospital.

Always a man of action, Rathmartin scribbled a note as soon as he got ashore, assuring his wife and two sons that all was well and requesting that they send another ship as soon as possible, for he'd heard of several recent mermaid sightings down off the north coast of Barbados and was most anxious to check into it. He had his traveling companion, the good Dr. Weimaraner, post the letter for him while he checked into the twelve-room Biscayne Hospital.

It was an untimely posting, however, for no sooner had Weimaraner left the Biscayne Post Office than our friend Josef Steinmetz showed up and retrieved the northbound mail on that fateful day, only to fling it with laughter out into the hot blue sea. Perhaps some day a few tattered fragments of the letter would wash up unnoticed on a beach in Long Island, carried there by the current of the Gulf Stream, but it would certainly never reach the offices of the Southwind company in Manhattan.

So Rathmartin waited, recovering at first, and then merely relaxing in the tropical environs. When he checked out of the hospital, he moved to a suite at the Biscayne Grand and rented a room for his doctor right next door. He began to relish the Florida tropics, the way he could wander just a few hundred yards up the beach and feel absolutely free of the encumbrances and responsibilities of civilization, yet still know, somewhere in the back of his mind, that there was a comfortable bed, a swimming pool, and a fully stocked bar just a stone's throw away. So, during the day, unbothered by the heat, Elias took long, boyish hikes up and down the beach, sometimes venturing a little ways into the bush, imagining that he was the sole shipwreck survivor on an island full of hungry cannibals and sensuous women. When the good doctor Weimaraner tagged along, Rathmartin referred to him as "Friday," and the doctor answered to it because he knew that somewhere in his contract there was probably a line that required him to do so. Then, each evening, they'd retire beside the swimming pool for some French cuisine and a bottle of Biscayne's best.

They waited, and still no ship came. But Elias Rathmartin was having such a time that he accepted the insult without the slightest hint of anger. "Well, Weimy," he'd say to the doctor, "no ship again today. I'll bet my boys have got things running so smoothly that every ship is out earning me profit." And the doctor would answer, "Yes, Admiral, I believe you're right," though inside he was fuming with impatience. The doctor was anxious to escape the heat and the mosquitoes and the mediocre service at the hotel, and he'd come to hate Rathmartin, because Rathmartin was the kind of man who wouldn't notice the heat or the service when he had other things to occupy him. And Rathmartin was the kind of man who didn't get bit by mosquitoes.

After five full weeks, a cruise ship finally came to port. It was a ship from a rival line, one that Rathmartin would never consider boarding. But he never missed an opportunity to engage in corporate spying, so he had Dr. Weimaraner sneak aboard under the pretense of booking passage.

The doctor returned with a handful of newspapers. "Look at this, Admiral," he said. "I found these scattered about the deck. Back copies of the *Times*."

Rathmartin thought for a moment. "What a capital idea, Friday. The news is old, of course, but it makes the passengers feel at home." He pulled on his mutton chops. "Yes, this is something to think about. Of course, we'd have to one-up them. What if we were to hire a paperboy, the sweetest little freckle-faced youngster we can get our hands on. Have him deliver the *Times* right to the door of their cabins. Bright and early. We'll tear off the dateline—after all, people don't care what day it is while they're at sea. If my boys are ambitious enough, they might even set up a little printing press on board and then we can print our own paper. Now, what do you think of a bicycle, Weimy? Can we get a boy skilled enough to ride a bicycle from cabin to cabin? Surely we can, and we'll get one of those quaint little children's bikes with lots of chrome and a little toot-horn. Are you getting this down, Weimy? My memory's not what it used to be, you know."

"I'm taking mental notes, Admiral. I'll write them down in my journal this evening."

"You might consider putting this in a letter to my sons if a Southwind ship doesn't arrive soon. This is an idea that can't wait."

"Yes, Admiral. I'll do that."

"Well, let's just have a peek at what's been happening back in the rotten old world of civilization, shall we?"

Rathmartin took a newspaper out of the doctor's hand and began to flip through the pages while he sipped his wine at their poolside table. The sun was just setting, and the ocean and sky in the east worked slowly toward a coordination of their nightly attire.

Rathmartin happened across the third installment of John Thomas's series on the new legend of the Barefoot Mailman. He was instantly hooked, and called for Dr. Weimaraner to hand over the other papers, one of which the doctor himself had been reading. Rathmartin read the series from start to finish, continuing to read even when it grew dark and the doctor led him by the elbow upstairs to their rooms. There, the magnate read by lamplight, late into the night, a sucker for all the thrills and adventure the reporter had injected into the tale. Suddenly, for the first time, he felt it was happening for real, all around him, that he was at last at the center of a unique and thrilling tropical adventure. After all, it was a true story. And here he was, by good fortune, smack in the middle of the best tale he'd ever read. He had to meet this man, this stoic mail carrier, for this was a man worthy of great admiration. This was a man who could be a true friend to Elias Rathmartin, who for so long had commanded a great fleet of ships and had loved and provided for a family, but who'd always felt misunderstood even by those closest to him. They'd laughed at his bent for high-seas romance and adventure, and yet they could never see that his business success and his thirst for adventure were one and the same. He was a man driven by an unquenchable yearning for something he could never quite put his finger on. *Just like this barefooted man from the town of Figulus,* he thought.

Chapter 16

THE NEXT MORNING, Rathmartin had Dr. Weimaraner inquire as to exactly where this little town was located and how they might travel there. The good doctor secured them a boat and a guide.

The guide's name was Chinasatuke, but she let the white people call her China—"like the dish," she'd say, because she didn't know about the country, and because when she'd been very young, she'd taken a white man for a lover and he'd told her, "You're quite a dish—a china dish," and she'd accepted that as a compliment. That was when she was fascinated by white people and hoped secretly that if she made love to enough white men she might just become white herself and leave behind the foolish ways of her tribe and of her parents, who treated her harshly and tried to keep her from straying outside the confines of their little village. But nothing could keep the young China from sneaking off in the night for a rendezvous with one of those bright-eyed soldier boys or a lonely pioneer, until at last she was caught, and when she tried to return to the village she was kicked and beaten. Her father said that if she wanted so much to be white she had no business living in a Seminole village, and so she was kicked out for good, with a few stones thrown at her back to make clear the village's feelings.

She laughed at their small-mindedness, and dreamed of the day when she'd ride through that village shooting her fancy white-man's gun in the air, with a hundred white soldiers to back her up, and take that village and make slaves of all the stupid Indians in it.

But when she went to her favorite lover and demanded that he marry her, he refused, and when he tried to make love to her, she kneed him in the testicles. She went from lover to lover, looking for the husband who could give her the last laugh, the husband who could make her white. But no one would take her hand in marriage, not even the sweetest of the bright-eyed soldier boys. She even lived with one for two years, hoping to change his mind. But still the man refused, and in the end she was left alone with no more lovers to knee in the testicles and not even a false promise to believe in.

When at last fear, hunger, and a need for acceptance of any kind outweighed her anger and her desire for revenge, she humbled herself and approached her old village, determined to accept the humiliation and the beatings if only she could regain some semblance of her old life. What she found was to change her completely: her old village was lifeless and rotting; many of her tribe had disappeared, and the rest lay slaughtered at the hands of the white troops, their bodies now exposed and decomposing in the shame of the bright sunlight on the flat, unconsecrated ground. There was her family's hut with the bodies of her parents and her little sister, who would now have been nearly of age to marry, all of them twisted unnaturally and covered with their own blood and the blood of each other.

She didn't cry; it was too horrible for that. Instead, she planted a seed of rage that she cultivated and nurtured until it became the sole purpose of her existence. It was this rage that gave her the will to survive the many years of lonely, hard times that followed. It was her mastery of this rage that allowed her to hide it completely and play out a plan that she knew could never work but whose execution was the only activity that truly gave her pleasure, now that she was forty-one and built like an overfed bear: to aid and encourage all white people down a path that would forever take them out of Florida. She could not frighten them all away, and she could not lead them out *en masse* like a pied piper, but she could show them the door one by one like a tired host at her own surprise party.

It was China who'd come by the Steinmetz residence the morning after that fateful night in the postmaster's restaurant. It was China who'd found the frightened Lena sitting at the table with the mosquito netting over her head and her face buried in her arms, bawling her eyes out. She'd said kind words to Lena and allayed her fears, then subtly and craftily convinced her that going home was the only thing to do. She'd paddled Lena all the way to the port in Biscayne and up to the dock where a Southwind steamer was anchored, and then showed her to the door of a first-class cabin that would take her back to Brooklyn. China had even made a down payment on that first-class cabin and an advance payment on a cabin for Lena's husband, in the hope that he'd show up and follow his wife home on the next departure. When China had later found out about Josef's capture in the Seminole village, she'd provided that information to the beachcombing pirates and convinced them that a rescue was in order. She'd known that the experience would then send Josef scurrying back north. And of course she'd been right.

Now the good doctor Weimaraner had offered China a generous sum of money to take him and Rathmartin to this little pioneer's town called Figulus, and China had accepted gladly, not for the money—which more than recouped her losses on deporting the Steinmetzes—but because she saw in this a first-rate opportunity to expose a wealthy and influential white man to such intense discomfort that he would never wish to return, and would, she hoped, relate this feeling to all his acquaintances and associates, so that with this one act she could prevent a hundred or more white profit seekers from turning their sights on Florida.

CHINA ROWED THEM up the coast, traveling the inner waterways when she could, and along the ocean's shore when the waves weren't too rough (she wanted them to be uncomfortable, but she didn't want to destroy her boat).

The doctor had horrible bouts of seasickness, particularly over the ocean, and spent much of the time with his head lolling over the side, retching at his own reflection. This pleased China no end. On the other hand, Rathmartin was pleasantly overwhelmed by the adventure of it and asked China a continuous stream of questions about the plants and wildlife and the Indian tribes. China would give him the Indian names and Rathmartin would repeat the words after her, then he'd glance over his shoulder—"Are you getting this, Friday?"—but the doctor's ears were full of the sound of his own retching, so Rathmartin would repeat the names again to commit them to memory, as if in doing so he were recreating the whole of Florida in his own image, or the image of the adventure books he'd read. It made China nervous to hear this white man speak Seminole words; it was as though, in addition to usurping their land, he wished to usurp the language and culture of her people as well. Then, when everything was finally stolen away from her people, when the white man owned the lands and the culture and all the memories of the Indians, her childhood dream would at last be fulfilled: she would become white. But now that dream filled her with rage and disgust, and it was only the great strength of her self-control that prevented her from strangling these white men and tossing them into the ocean. Much later, she'd regret that she hadn't.

THE SKIFF PULLED up to the dock in front of the Figulus post office on the second day. There was no one to be seen in town, but from the docks they could hear some talking and laughter down the path.

"There must be some sort of town meeting," said Rathmartin. "Perhaps their relations with the savages have come to a crisis and they're taking up arms. We've come at just the right time, Weimy. China, you'd better remain in the boat. If any of them question you, just tell them you're employed faithfully to Elias Rathmartin and the Southwind Trading Company."

"But they may not know who you are back here in the jungle, Admiral," said the doctor, still green in the face, but slowly regaining some strength.

"Good point, Weimy. Perhaps it's best if you hide on the floor of the boat, China."

"Yes," said China, having no intention of hiding from anyone.

With that, they left China behind and walked toward the voices of the townsfolk, arriving shortly at the torchlit entrance to Earl Shank's restaurant.

Chapter 17

MELY HAD DONE A beautiful job of fixing up the restaurant. Everything was polished to a dull, woody shine. The tables were set just like a fancy restaurant, with more silverware at each place than any local person knew how to use. Each table had a candle and a vase with flowers and even some flowered napkins she'd made out of old drapery. Earl was pleasantly surprised that Mely had it in her to transform the restaurant this way; it looked fancier than he'd ever imagined possible. The only thing it lacked was a steady flow of customers. But that would change, he thought, because as he wedged himself into his new loafers, he had the warmest feeling of hope and self-confidence. He had no idea how, but he knew that tonight the future would unfold before him like a red carpet, and that these fine leather shoes would provide the missing dance steps in his waltz to fame.

He kept himself and the shoes hidden from Mely until the guests started to show. When people came to the door, some as singles, some as couples, some with a couple of kids, the first thing they noticed was the mellow glow of Earl's new shoes in the lamplight.

"Nice shoes, Earl," they'd say, and when Mely first heard them say it, she peeked across the room and down at Earl's feet. She could only shake her head.

"I won't even ask, Earl."

"I ain't stole 'em, Mely," he said, but she kept shaking her head with that look that told Earl she'd put up with him anyway.

The restaurant filled up quickly. They were only townsfolk who'd come for a free meal of pig roast, but for Earl it was a preview of the success to come. It was good practice, he thought.

As Earl was seating the last of the guests, Mely started for the kitchen to check on the roast. She stopped, though, when she glanced to the door and spotted two men she'd never seen before in her life—a burly old man with frizzy muttonchops, and a balding, middle-aged man with a black doctor's bag. She went to the door.

"Can I help you gentlemen?"

"Madam, I am Elias J. Rathmartin, and this is my good man, Dr. Renaldo Weimaraner. We are charmed to make your acquaintance." He bowed ever so slightly.

"If you all are a couple of carpetbaggers, you come to the wrong place to sell yer hocus-pocus."

"Yes, my apologies for our appearance. We have just navigated up from the Biscayne Grand Hotel. The good doctor doesn't travel well in small boats, and I am just an old man. But in my remaining hours on this earth, I seek what small adventures are left for us doddering fools, and I have come here to gain audience with this courageous young wanderer I have heard so much of, this Barefoot Mailman."

Mely looked at him as if she'd just identified the missing ingredient in her stew. "Earl," she said, looking over her shoulder. "Earl," she said, a little louder now.

Earl pulled himself away from the tables where he was playing host and hurried up to the door when he spotted Mely with the strangers.

"Earl," said Mely, "these men are looking for you," and then she turned toward the kitchen, washing her hands of the matter.

166

"Yes sirs," said Earl. "What kin I do fer ya?"

Rathmartin looked down at Earl's feet.

"I can't blame ya fer looking," laughed Earl. "These are the finest shoes in the South. I ain't embarrassed to say it neither, since these shoes were delivered to me out of the clear blue, like God's gift to a hardworkin pioneer, if it ain't too blasphemous fer me to say so."

"Those are fine shoes indeed," said Rathmartin. "But I'm not sure you're the one we're looking for, despite what your wife says."

"Oh, don't pay her no mind. She just ain't used to dealin with the upper crust. A little shy, ya understand."

"Yes, certainly. But we've come looking for someone— hand me that paper, won't you, Weimy?"

The doctor pulled a copy of the *Times* from his medical bag. Rathmartin presented it to Earl.

"My name, though I see now it holds no weight here in the dark jungles of Florida, is Elias J. Rathmartin, and I'm looking for this Barefoot Mailman everyone is talking about."

The old man's name carried Earl back to his very brief stint in the shipping business. Even then, Elias Rathmartin was respected and feared among his competitors. Earl realized he was talking to one of the richest, most powerful Yankees in the country.

He took the newspaper. "Barefoot Mailman, huh? Well, I . . ." He began to scan the first installment of John Thomas's already legendary story, recognizing with a shock the striking similarity to his lost friend, Josef Steinmetz. But Earl didn't puzzle over it for long. For him, the story quickly became more than just strange coincidence, more than just a self-serving lie told by an opportunistic, fame-hungry reporter. For Earl, the story was a ticket out of a lifetime of failures, it was a fortuitous juxtaposition of heavenly bodies, a hand-out from the gods.

"Wellsir," said Earl, "you come to the right place. That barefoot feller comes in here all the time. He's a good friend of mine. See, let me innerduce myself—my name's Earl Shank." He shook both their hands and felt the pulse of fortune electrifying the moment. He'd rehearsed for one role his entire life, and now, out of nowhere, an agent had come who had the power and the money to land him that role. Things were set in motion, and all because of the shoes. "I'm the postmaster in this town, that's how I know 'im so well. And this here's my restaurant, where I invite him to sup when he ain't out deliverin the mail in his bare feet. I know it ain't the fanciest restaurant, but he's a simple sorter feller, he is. Sits by himself at that back table right over there. Don't talk much, just sorts through the mail, counts it, makes sure he don't lose none of it. He's real serious about his job, and always has a real serious look on his face, like he's workin out some plan ta save the world. He's friendly, though, once ya get to know 'im as well as I do. An he likes the food here, I'm proud ta say that. My wife's been called the finest cook south of Atlanta, and—well, if ya got time, maybe ya'd like to sample fer yerselves. She's cooked up a special pig roast, with some sorter citrus sauce—she won't never tell me what she puts in it. I'll sit ya right there, where he sits, and if he happens to show up—and ya never know when he might—why I'll just bring 'im right to ya, innerduce ya, sit 'im right there at yer table. He'll do it fer me."

"Well, Friday, I believe we've met a friend among the savages. Sir, we'd be honored by your hospitality."

"Wait here, just a moment." Earl hurried over to the table he'd pointed at, which was currently occupied by the Bardo family—Frank and Edna and their daughters Lisa and Lila. He whispered to Frank that he'd given them the wrong table, that this here table was reserved for an honored guest from out of town.

"But there ain't no other table, Earl," said Frank.

Earl apologized, but said he had to ask Frank and his family to come back next time and dinner would be on the house. And anyway, he'd have Mely bring by the leftovers tomorrow morning—that roasted pig always tasted better the second day, when the juices had settled and the flavors aged.

"Well you kin jest ferget it, Earl. It wouldn't be right for us to accept somthin from people who treat us like dirt." Frank got his family up from the table and they marched out of the restaurant in a huff. The girls were crying.

Earl knew he was going to have to apologize profusely tomorrow. But tomorrow, everything would be different.

Although they were the last to arrive, Elias Rathmartin and Dr. Weimaraner were the first to be served, and, unlike the other guests, were presented with a bottle of wine, mostly full, that Earl had taken from Mely's private cooking stock. The townsfolk did not fail to notice this, and began to grumble about Earl's catering to the rich Yankees.

"What's he want from them Yankees, anyway?"

"I wouldn't want to be too nice to them folks. They might come back."

"An bring more with 'em."

"An they's plenty more where they came from."

"I curse the day that I've lived this long to see a Southern man grovel before a fat-cat Yankee carpetbagger."

"It's them Yankee shoes Earl got. They done turned him into a Yankee!"

"I wouldn't mind being no Yankee if I had me a pair a shoes like that!"

"Keep yer mouth shut, boy."

They were a little angry and frightened by this Yankee invasion, but they also couldn't help feeling honored by the presence of such distinguished gentlemen, though they'd never admit to it.

Earl played the obsequious waiter to the pair of Yankees and didn't seem to hear the complaints of his neighbors. They got their food in time, and when everyone had Mely's pork with citrus sauce stuffed happily into their mouths, they quickly forgot Earl's injustices and forgave him his foolishness. That was just Mayor Earl up to his old tricks again. How could they get upset about that?

Everything was going smoothly for Earl, as if the event had been rehearsed a thousand times over and revised in the process to iron out the kinks. The restaurant looked and sounded like he'd always imagined it would, and he had complete confidence that the day would soon come when every night would be just like this, only the local clientele would be replaced by more and more rich Yankees, praises rolling off their tongues and bankrolls out of their pockets. Like red carpets.

But there was one thing he couldn't have counted on, and like a demonic apparition, that one thing soon made its appearance in the doorway. Earl stopped in midstride when he saw him, and then the guests stopped chewing and looked at him, too. The entire restaurant silenced itself in nervous tension. The man stood in the doorway, his face grizzled, his clothes tattered, and his lips quivering with malice. Earl had seen him only once before, but recognized him as the mail carrier whom Josef Steinmetz had replaced. He'd nearly ruined Earl's life before when he'd punched Josef in the face, and here he'd come to try it again.

The man had learned of his dismissal when he'd wandered into the Biscayne Post Office a few days after Josef Steinmetz. Furious, he'd gone on a drunken rampage and tried to set fire to the post office, the city hall, and several beachfront hotels. Fortunately, none of the fires took hold, but he did spend several days in jail for violating the new law about urinating on the beach. In those sober moments in the Biscayne jail, he vowed to investigate any and all persons responsible for his joblessness.

Now, his investigations complete, he had come to seek revenge. He spotted Earl across the small room and pointed a finger at him. "You stinkin son of a bitch," he said.

Earl dropped the tray of dirty plates he was holding and put himself behind a table.

"You Yankee-lovin sewer rat," he continued, taking an un-steady step in Earl's direction and shaking his fist. "You put me out of a job 'cause I did what any respectable Southern man ought to do when he meets a Yankee. And then you re-placed me with some half-breed Injun."

"I got no idear what yer talkin about, mister," said Earl, from behind Josh McCready's table. "Now why don't you run along and find another pint a that whisky I can smell from clear over here."

"Don't lie to me, Injun-lover. I read all about it in the *New York Times*. You replaced *me*—a hard-workin up-standin Southern man—with a dirty Injun savage." Then he ad-dressed the whole restaurant, as if he'd just noticed he had an audience. "Jes when we finally beat them cannibal savages back into the swamps, this Injun-lover decides ta start hirin the red devils to deliver our mail. Tell me, who here wants a dirty savage handlin the letters we send to our mothers and ladyfriends?"

The townsfolk shook their heads, mumbling words to the effect of "Not us."

"And he puts loyal Southerners outta work ta do it. I tell ya, this man's infiltratin the U.S. Gov'ment with bloody sav-ages and means ta give back what we all worked so hard ta take. Why? 'Cause he wants ta be king a the savages, I tell ya. King a the bloody red devils. He wants ta woo-woo aroun a big berlin' pot with yer heads in it. Well, you good folks know what we do with heathen cannibals, don't ya? We string 'em up and watch their bloody red cannibal tongues roll outta their heads. An that's what we oughtta do here tonight."

Earl feared for his life. He saw in the eyes around him a re-flection of the unjust service he'd given them tonight, and he suddenly knew how little it takes for a man to be hanged, how the little wrongs he'd done to a dozen people suddenly be-come one big wrong when those people start thinking with the same mind. And though it is true that any self-respecting Southern town would have been stirred to action by such words, the inert soul of Figulus could not be dragged so easily from under its rock. They all looked at each other and mumbled words to the effect of "Mmm."

Fortunately for Earl, Elias Rathmartin was there. He'd heard it all, and he had had enough. He rose from his chair to address the ex–mail carrier.

"You have no business talking to our host this way. I know the story of which you speak, and this man did the right thing in hiring that barefoot lad. Why, I don't believe you read the story at all. In fact, I doubt you even know how to read. The man you say took your place is no half-breed Indian, he's a full-blooded American lad who had the misfortune to fall in with savages after his family was killed in a shipwreck. If anyone doubts me, I have the complete five-part series here in my good doctor's medical bag. Now, I don't know why you were replaced, sir, but I think I can guess." He addressed the entire room now. "Look at this man. Is this whiskey-drinking, foulmouthed ruffian the man you want as a representative of the United States Postal Service?"

Someone spoke up boldly, "No!"

"Why, this man isn't good enough to lick our boots," continued Rathmartin. "It's clear to me that, whatever his reasons at the time, your gracious host and postmaster did the right thing in replacing this smelly monster. From what I know of him, the man who took his place is the finest example of courageous American youth I've yet to lay eyes on. *This* man has no business here. I don't say we lynch him, because that's the kind of lawlessness that belongs to men of his own kind. But a good tarring and feathering ought to teach him not to disturb the good people of this town again."

The townsfolk were mesmerized by Rathmartin's speech. A few even clapped.

The ex-postman was enraged and stepped up to Rathmartin's table, fists clenched and yellow teeth gritted.

"Who the hell do you think you are? Yankee! You another one a this Yankee-lover's Yankee friends?"

"No!" shouted Earl from across the room, having seen once before what was coming.

"Sir, if it means anything to you, I am Elias J. Rathmartin of New York."

"He's lying!" shouted Earl, pushing aside tables and trying to leap between the two men. "He's from Georgia!"

"Well, Mr. New York," said the ex-postman, "welcome to Florida," and he smashed his fist into Rathmartin's face.

Rathmartin fell back into his doctor's lap, holding his eye. Earl got there just in time to wonder if there was still some way he could turn back what had happened, for it was certain to destroy his promising and advantageous relationship with the shipping magnate. He helped the doctor lift Rathmartin into his chair. He put his hands on Rathmartin's head, brushed the hair out of Rathmartin's blackening eye, moaning, "Oh no, oh no." But when he turned to call Mely for a wet towel or a piece of meat, he saw only the ex-postman's fist, and the last thing he remembered that night was the taste of those salty knuckles.

Chapter 18

W HEN EARL AWOKE the next morning, his wife had a mirror
ready and put it in front of his face. His nose was bloody,
his teeth framed in red, and his upper lip split.

"I'm not gonna say ya deserve it, Earl, but ya ought to know
better'n ta stop a drunken maniac with yer face."

"Where's that millionaire feller?" said Earl thickly, pushing himself up in bed. "Rathmartin."

"He left early this morning. Said he had to catch a boat
down in Biscayne."

"How could you let 'im go without me apoligizin? You
can't let a millionaire slip through yer hands like that. He
could make us rich, Mely, and famous."

"Earl, I got no desire to be rich and famous, specially at my
age." She cut a piece of bandage to put on Earl's lip. "Anyway,
he said he'd be in touch."

"Yeah, he likely wants to sue me."

"He can sue all he wants: we ain't got nothing to give him."

Mely washed and bandaged Earl's poor face while he yelped
and winced in pain. He knew she was right. *But if he was to
sue us*, he thought, *there'd be some publicity in that*. Still, he
might just have let the opportunity of a lifetime slip through
his hands. His mediocrity, which he'd for so long held as an

asset, might just have doomed him to a full life of inconsequentiality.

RATHMARTIN AND THE doctor reached Biscayne the next day, thanks to the speedy paddling of China, who could smell their desire to leave. There, they found a Southwind trader docked in the port. Rathmartin had a throbbing headache and a fine pair of shiners that made him look demonic, so that, when he boarded his ship, the crew stood back, curious and a little frightened. He went straight to the captain and demanded to know what had taken him so long to get here. The captain explained that he was on his regular trading route, that he had no idea Mr. Rathmartin was in Florida, but that Mr. Rathmartin's sons mentioned that he, the captain, might inquire after their father while he, the captain, was in the Caribbean, since Mr. Rathmartin had been away for several weeks without communication.

"Without communication?!"

Rathmartin was furious that his letter had not reached its destination, and he cursed the United States Postal Service for its ineptitude, and himself for inquiring after such a dull-witted character as this Barefoot Mailman. If the man could not get one simple, lightweight letter to its proper destination, then what kind of example was he setting for other young carriers—indeed, the whole of America's youth? Anyway, what kind of man would be foolish enough to walk such long distances in his bare feet? Why, there must be something not right in the man's brain.

"May I ask what happened to your face, sir?"

"No, Captain, you may not." As soon as Rathmartin spoke, though, he realized he'd let his discomfort and his anger get the better of him. He was being a foolish old geezer. When he calmed himself, he began to recall the events at the restaurant in a different light. There was the pain, of course, and the embarrassment, but when he looked at it objectively, the event seemed like something out of one of his adventure novels—

he'd been there, to a little saloon in the midst of a tropical jungle. He'd mingled with the locals and won their admiration with his bravery and his oratory skills. True, he was scarred from the experience, but no man passes through the dark, wild jungle unscathed by her needley claws. At least he'd left there sitting up in his boat, which is more than he could say for that drunken Johnny Reb. Of course, he'd got a little help in that regard from his oversized Indian guide—she'd heard the ruckus in the restaurant and presented herself on the scene just in time to catch the reb's fist before it struck him again—she'd twisted it back and knocked him out cold. Then how the whole town had laughed and cheered when that drunk was put back in his skiff and shoved off into Lake Worth, feet first, with his tongue lolling out of his mouth. But Rathmartin had thanked his Indian enough for all that, and she'd seemed all too happy to pound an Indian-hater to the ground. So there was no real need to thank her publicly. The key to a good story is what you leave out, after all.

"Actually, Captain," said Rathmartin, "if you pour me a drink, I'll tell you a good story."

Rathmartin continued to tell the story all the way back to New York, and when they arrived there, he told the story some more—to his friends and family, and most of all to the Explorer's Club, where he was quickly made a most respected member, not only for his adventurous exploits, but for his ability to tell a ripping good story about them.

The story was so popular with everyone he told it to that one day it came to him: if so many people enjoyed a good adventure tale, why not let them live it? Southwind Cruise Lines was experiencing intense competition from the Norwegian lines and from Cunard, both of which had added new routes for pleasure cruises to Florida and the Caribbean. So he briefly turned his attention away from his personal quest for adventure and made the last and what he considered the most brilliant business decision of his life. When he'd set the idea down on paper, he summarized it in a letter to the postmaster of Figulus.

EARL WAS IN limbo while he let his face heal. He'd lost control again and let fortune slip through his hands. Now anything could happen. The question was, Who had absconded with his fortune? And in what condition would it be returned? If the millionaire carried it, it might return in the form of a lawsuit or a wrecking crew to level his little restaurant. If that drunken ex-carrier had it, it might return again and again in the form of a fist. And what if that huge Indian woman had taken it? She could crush it as she'd crushed that drunk's face. And who knows what sinister ceremonies those Injuns could perform to shape his destiny toward their own ends? The Injuns knew about things like that; they knew the power of the unseen. And that scared him.

For many weeks Earl waited. He sat all day in the shadows of the bedroom and waited for the world to come crashing through his door. He left the house just once a week to perform his postmaster's duties, which he did in dread of finding the fateful letter that would spell out his ruin. Certain enough, a letter arrived addressed to the postmaster and postmarked in New York City. It wasn't at all what he expected.

With trembling fingers, he read the personal letter from Elias Rathmartin, scrawled on Southwind letterhead. He read each word more than once, because it took that much to get the meaning through to his paralyzed and unbelieving brain. When he finally set it down, he rushed out of the post office, leaving the unsorted mail on the counter, and ran along the banks of the lake to Mely's little garden behind their house.

"Mely," he yelled. "We done it! We finally done it!"

He showed her the letter, which explained how Rathmartin was going to make Figulus a regular stop on Southwind's cruises to Biscayne. Biscayne was all right, Rathmartin said, but its refinement made it too much like the North. His idea was to give his passengers a taste of what the Florida wilderness was really like. He wanted everyone to know the excitement and also the hardships that pioneers such as Mr. Shank experience on a daily basis. The ships would anchor off the inlet at the north end of the lake, and passengers would then be ferried through the inlet and down the shore of Lake Worth to the town of Figulus, where they would meet with real pioneers and sample the local flavors at Mr. Shank's restaurant.

The letter enclosed a contract detailing the plan and also stating how much Earl would be paid per customer. A few quick calculations made Earl's heart leap into his throat and he squeezed the breath out of his wife.

"This is it!" he shouted. "We're going to be famous. And that's just for starters!" He hopped from foot to foot, and when he let her go he did a little jig, swinging his arms and crossing his feet with astonishing coordination for a big man, as though he'd practiced for it all his life.

Mely smiled, trying to catch her breath. She was happy for him, but also a little bit dazed and frightened. Things like this didn't happen to anyone she knew, and she'd never expected anything from Earl except big, boyish dreams and the healthy lies he'd tell himself when they didn't work out. It all seemed unreal to her, like she'd entered someone else's fairy tale, like Earl had finally created such a complex and overwrought fantasy that he'd succeeded in pulling her into it, making her believe for a moment it was real. She fully expected to snap out of it after a good night's rest. She hoped she would, too, because as marvelous as this fantasy world was, it was just too different and scary for a simple woman like herself.

Earl never doubted it for a minute. When he finally returned to his room that night, after telling everyone in town the good news, he took out the loafers he hadn't worn since he'd been punched out in his own restaurant. He'd been afraid they'd put some sort of curse on him. But now he took a rag and dusted them off and buffed them to a shine, so that he could see his big smile in the cherry brown leather. *My fortune never left me at all*, he thought. *It was right here all the time, smiling away under the dust I let collect on these here lucky shoes. Well, I'll never let that shine dull again, and I'll never be so foolish as to take off my lucky shoes.*

Chapter 19

THINGS BEGAN TO happen quickly for Earl, too quickly for him to think much about them. When Rathmartin received the signed contract, he immediately sent Earl a sizable advance to cover the costs of expansions and renovations to the restaurant. Up to this point, most of the town had been skeptical and wary of this new development. The last thing they wanted was a bunch of rich old Yankees invading their solitude. But when Earl hired them all to help with the renovations and the decorations, the objections somehow slipped their minds. Even the Bardos, who had remained cool to Earl after they'd been kicked out of their restaurant seats to make room for the two Yankees, somehow found forgiveness in their hearts when they saw that money was being passed around. "Earl's a man with foresight," said Frank Bardo. "We got ta rally behind him and move this town into the twentieth century."

When the renovations were complete and the town waited for the first ship to arrive, people got to thinking about how they might get a piece of this action. It wasn't fair for Earl to get all the money; those rich old Yankees had more than enough for everyone. So it wasn't long before Figulus became the arts-and-crafts capital of Florida. The men sat around on their front porches all day, whittling out Indians and seagulls from blocks of pinewood, or designing little craft stands to be set up somewhere along the route those rich Yankees would walk between the new dock and the renovated restaurant, now called "Postmaster General's Tropical Outpost, Fine Dining, Earl and Mely Shank, Props." The women of the town crocheted little wallhangings with biblical quotes on them and sewed together shirts with leaping fish on them, and baby clothes with happy alligators. Suddenly, the town had a singleness of purpose, a community feeling that warmed Earl's heart. It was an unexpected side effect of the fulfillment of Earl's dream. In Earl's mind, even before the first boatload of Yankees docked in front of the post office, the little town of Figulus had become a sort of Paradise on Earth.

THE WEALTHY YANKEES came as Earl had promised, and the town settled into a weekly routine. Two days before the boat arrived, the sewing and whittling would heat up rapidly, and the town would transform itself into a tropical Santa's workshop for Yankee tourists. On Tuesdays, when the boat arrived, people busied themselves with fixing up their little craft stands and arranging their merchandise to show off their finest, most expensive work. Earl would dress himself up and wedge himself as far as he could into his lucky loafers while Mely started the cooking. About 4:30, two small ferries would pull up to the dock, and Mayor Earl himself would greet the guests one by one, then take them *en masse* to his restaurant, pausing in front of the craft stands that faced the lake. On average, there were about twenty-five tourists, sometimes as many as thirty. Mely had the meals all prepared, and the guests were served shortly after they were seated. There was no menu; it was family-style dining. The guests ate it up and loved every minute of the experience. Then, maybe an hour later, they were brought back by the craft stands, where they lingered for another fifteen minutes, oohing and aahing and buying the carvings and wallhangings at inflated prices. Finally, they were whisked up the lake and out the inlet in their ferries.

The whole event took maybe two hours, but enough money was spent in that time to throw the town into wild celebration for the next two days, particularly if someone got hold of some whiskey. People in Figulus had finally been pulled out of their drowsy homes. They learned to dance and sing and tell an occasional joke. If it weren't that their entire lives were centered around wringing money from wealthy tourists, one might even imagine them to be a town of regular folk. They were all getting rich, especially because they didn't have much to spend their money on. They made trips up to Fort Pierce and down to Biscayne sometimes and picked up some new clothes or a new boat, but mostly they just collected money and took much joy in passing it around at the dinner table, touching it and holding it and counting it and talking about all the things they could buy with it.

For the tourists, the town of Figulus and Postmaster General's was a unique and exotic experience. Even the members of Rathmartin's Explorer's Club were impressed. The restaurant felt to them like a dose of Southern hospitality in the midst of a forbidding tropical wilderness. Though the wine wasn't as good as the wine in the Biscayne resorts, the postmaster fawned on his guests in a manner they were unaccustomed to in haughtier environs. Earl was the ingratiating native who symbolized for his guests the quaint and carefree Florida lifestyle, particularly, they said, in the way he wore his fine leather shoes like a pair of slippers, untucked in the back and flapping against his bare heels. The restaurant experience was so unique that they just had to buy something to commemorate it, or no one back in New York, or in Connecticut or Massachusetts could possibly believe them.

The sun shined on the little town, and times were good. Indeed, Earl Shank himself could ask for little more. Though he didn't need the money, he kept his job as postmaster for the sole reason that it highlighted the magnitude of his success.

He'd used to sit at his counter and daydream about all his schemes to achieve the fortune he deserved, or else moan and sigh about his continual failure to see them through; now it pleased him no end to sit at that same counter, sorting mail and reminding himself that his plans had been a success, that *he* was a success. It wasn't gloating, but a warm, almost religious feeling of bliss. Beatitude. Perhaps his only regret was that it was all happening so fast. He wished he could slow things down and enjoy each blissful moment as something unto itself.

Then one Friday, while basking in the grace of just such a blissful moment, Earl was rudely awakened. Silas Lautermilch, the current mail carrier, arrived to drop off some letters that had come through Biscayne and to take the few that were destined for the outside world. The retired seaman always stayed over to chat Earl's ear off with gossip from other parts of the coast.

On this occasion, he told Earl that he ought to feel lucky he had him as his carrier. Not because he was the best carrier in the business—he wouldn't be so vain as to say any such thing. But other postmasters up and down the coast were having all kinds of problems keeping carriers on the job these days, what with all the ghost stories floating about.

"What ghost stories?" asked Earl.

"Don't tell me you ain't heard. Ever since that last carrier disappeared, people been tellin stories, sayin they seen 'im walkin the beach at night—seen 'is ghost I ought ta say. They say he looks like 'e's already been ta hell and back—'e's got two black eyes, and a purple nose, and walks sorta hunched over like this—like 'e's got chains around 'is neck. Oh, and I almost forgot, he ain't got no shoes on. I guess 'e's one a them barefoot mailmen people are always talking about, though I hain't never seen a carrier in 'is right mind 'ould walk a route without no shoes. Hell, I don't even do much walkin, but I wouldn't sit out there in the sun all day without nothin to cover m'foots, not even in a boat. No sir, I can't say I b'lieve in no barefoot mailmen. In all confidentchality, I think folks're gettin 'em mixed up with a tribe of Injuns. But ghosts, now them's a different story. A fella cain't deny they's ghosts, especially a fella like me who's seen 'em, though I hain't never seen a land ghost, jest a sea ghost—late at night when yer on a watch, and somthin draws yer eyes up to the crow's nest, somthin that glows, with eyes big as night, or else right at dusk, when the sun sinks into the ocean, you get that green flash, and they say that's all the sea ghosts wakin up, that when the sun hits 'em jest right, they all wake up at once and rise from the ocean ta do their hauntin duties for the night."

Right away, Earl thought, *I know why his ghost walks the beach. I know who he's lookin for.* A shudder ran up his spine. Why had this man and his ghost stories come to disperse the holy mist of his success? He'd have to shake this off.

"I reckon I don't take no stock in ghost stories," said Earl.

"Suit yerself, but lots of folks say they seen 'im. An they say he ain't barefoot by choice. No sir, someone stole 'is shoes, and that's who he's lookin for, they say. He walks up and down the coast ever night, lookin for the fella that stole 'is shoes. That postmaster down in Biscayne specalates that he requires them shoes to make the ard'ous climb to heaven. I ain't so sure. Maybe so. What you think a dead man wants with a pair a shoes?"

Some frightening visions were creeping into Earl's thoughts, almost against his will. "I tole ya I don't take no stock in ghost stories," he said. "I don' keer what a dead man wants. He's dead and he ain't gonna get 'em."

"Suit yerself," shrugged the carrier, picking up his mail sack. "But if I was you, I'd carry an extra pair of shoes with me if I happened to take a evenin stroll on the beach. You cain't be too sure, that's what I always says. Course, you wouldn't want to take them fancy loafers you got."

When the carrier left, Earl tried to convince himself the story was bunk. *I don't take no stock in ghost stories,* he thought, but it didn't seem to help, and his stomach knotted and his teeth bit into his thumb when he recalled the carrier's words: "What you think a dead man wants with a pair a shoes?" The old salt had spun off that tale like it was another big fish story. But then, the carrier had nothing to fear; he wasn't wearing a dead man's shoes.

Chapter 20

ALL THE WARMTH and satisfaction that Earl had enjoyed the last few months crumbled away as his superstitions got the better of him. That night, when he tried to sleep, his heart tightened and his eyes bulged at every croak, chirp, rustle, and thump that leapt out of the darkness at him.

"Did you hear that?"

"I heard you, making a racket there."

"I thought I heard footsteps, Mely."

"Then why don't you get up and check. But be quiet about it."

"No, no," he said. "It must have been nothing. Sorry to wake you, hon."

He cast a glance at the loafers, just beneath the window in the pool of moonlight that gave them an eerie glow. When he gained just a little courage, he stretched a foot out of bed and kicked them into the darkness.

"Quiet, Earl," said Mely.

In the morning he couldn't bring himself to wear the loafers. Since he'd considered his old shoes an embarrassment to even have in the same house with the loafers, and so had thrown them away, he didn't have any shoes to wear. Sure, he had plenty of money for new shoes, but he didn't have the time now to travel to a store in Biscayne or Fort Pierce, and he didn't have the courage to provide an explanation to someone who might make the purchase for him. So he hid the shoes under the bed and went barefoot.

He told Mely that he just wanted to let the shoes air for a while. She looked at him funny, but didn't say anything. When he went to the post office and folks came in and asked what had happened to those famous shoes of his, he replied that Mely was polishing them for him. But when the questions persisted for a few days, he allowed that he'd had to send the shoes to New York to be polished professionally, since no one in Florida was qualified to handle leather of such high quality.

Still, hiding the shoes did nothing to diminish his fright. At the first hint of dusk, his body tensed and his brow sweated, his mind became a turmoil of imagined evil.

Worst of all were the nights when the Yankee tourists came. Earl became a nuisance to his guests, spilling wine and dropping plates as he imagined an apparition floating by the window or footsteps padding the roof. People began to talk. The guests mumbled among themselves about the ineptness of the service and the unsanitary conditions of the restaurant. Quaintness is one thing, they said, but a waiter with bare feet is stretching the limit. And what filthy, ill-formed feet besides. And now that they thought about it, the food wasn't as good as they'd been led to believe.

It wasn't long before this sort of talk made its way back to New York and was passed around in the highest social circles. Southwind Cruise Lines suffered a steep falling off of business on their Florida and Caribbean routes. The Yankee guests in Figulus slowed to a trickle and the whole town suffered.

At first, Earl thought he could attribute it to the end of the season. It was spring, now, and the weather was beginning to heat up. There was no snow for the Yankees to escape, and there was no reason for them to put up with the insects and the Florida sun that seemed to grow bigger and hotter by the day. Soon, though, Earl would know that it wasn't just the season.

When the first quarter reports came in and were analyzed thoroughly, the Rathmartin boys were forced to make some hard decisions. As usual, their father, Elias, was off on one of his adventure-tale fantasies, so they made their decisions without his advice or knowledge. It was the first really big decision they'd made without their father around, and they were proud of themselves for making it—proud to consult their lawyers and their board of vice presidents, proud to have their secretaries draft up the letter addressed to Earl Shank from the Directors of the Southwind Company.

Dear Mr. Shank,
    This is to inform you in writing, as per article three, paragraph one of our contract, that the Southwind Cruise Lines hereby renders null and void said contract, with the stated reason of a downturn in business resulting from the word-of-mouth of recent cruise guests dissatisfied with their experience in your restaurant. Statistical evidence will be provided if you so request it.
    Cordially,
    Stanislaw and Merwyn Rathmartin, Directors
    The Southwind Cruise Lines and Shipping and
    Trading Company

Earl read this letter five or six times, then wandered out of his post office in a daze. *It's them damned, cursed shoes*, he thought. But he knew that it wasn't just the shoes, either.

He wandered into his house and past Mely.

"What's wrong, Earl?" she asked, looking up from a new recipe she was experimenting with.

Earl didn't answer her. He shuffled into the bedroom and dug around under the bed until he found the cursed shoes. He held them with his pinkies, afraid something evil might rub off. Then he walked past Mely again and out the door.

She called after him, trying to rib him and lighten his mood, "Earl, you get your shoes back from New York?"

No answer.

He went down to the dock and borrowed Josh McCready's skiff, setting the shoes as far away from him in the boat as possible, careful not to disturb them or shake them up too much for fear of angering whatever evil powers they held. Still, he knew it wasn't just the shoes; he had to blame himself.

He rowed steadily, huffing and puffing, his belly getting in the way of the oars. In a little while he was across the lake, and when he beached the boat and took out the shoes, he found that he'd washed up in front of what must have been Josef Steinmetz's home. There was the little shack with the covered porch and the rocking chairs for him and his wife. Just to the north, he spotted the burned-out orchard, some life finally beginning to take root around the black, skeletal remains of the citrus trees. He went up and sat for a while on one of those rocking chairs on the porch. He had the emptiest feeling, as if all his success of the past few months had been only a lot of hot air in his balloon, and now he'd found the leak, the widening hole.

He felt closer to that immigrant than ever, even if the man was dead, and even if his ghost was seeking Earl out to frighten him to death. He deserved it. Just like Earl, Josef Steinmetz was a man who'd seen his misty dreams blown off by an evil wind. He was a man who'd had his hopes slapped away by the cool hand of fate. But Earl knew there was one key difference: with Earl, it wasn't just the shoes and it wasn't just fate; it was his own foolishness. He'd let the whole town down, he'd let Mely down, and he'd let himself down. Again. He could handle the jabs of the townsfolk—they'd made fun of him before, and it almost seemed just that they'd do it again. And he knew that Mely would forgive him—she hadn't been completely convinced of their success yet, anyway. But for himself, this seemed like the final defeat, one he could not forget. He'd finally got what he'd always wanted, and then by his own foolishness and superstition, he'd let it slip away. There was no use blaming it on the shoes, though he didn't doubt there was something unearthly about them—his fate had been tied too closely to them for it to be pure chance.

But whether by the magic of the shoes or not, he'd finally been given the starring role in the performance of his own happy fortune—not a role many men receive, or if they do, not one they recognize they're playing. And he'd blown it— he'd blown the lines, he'd used all the wrong gestures, and he'd dragged the show down after a promising opening. Now he'd never act in this town again. No one would let him; he was no longer convincing as anything but a fool. He no longer had the confidence to try any of the challenging and entertaining roles he'd played before. There was nothing else for him to do now, nothing else to look forward to, but to wade his way out into the ocean and muster the last of his abilities together to play the Final Role—the role with no audience, the role for which there'd be no applause and no re- views, nothing but the satisfaction of one role well played— for there was only one way to play it—and then that final fall of the curtain.

He'd be missed, but only until next Tuesday, when the Yan- kee cruise ship would not anchor off the inlet, and the Yankee tenders would not dock in front of the post office, and the Yan- kee millionaires would not spend any money on the quaint lit- tle souvenir trinkets. Then they'd know. Mely would cry, but she was strong, and she'd get over him just like she got over ol' Jake, though he hoped it would take longer than the five weeks she took to get over him. Then his absence would be covered up and smoothed over until people forgot him alto- gether, except for once or twice when they were sitting alone on their porches, staring at the sunset, and just for a second they'd remember the few months of good times that Mayor Earl brought to Figulus, and they'd say to themselves, *Those were the days*, but they'd never say anything out loud, because it wouldn't be appropriate to talk about it. And that was okay with Earl, because that was all he could hope for now—that someone would remember him fondly, if only for a moment, and think about what he'd tried to do.

Well that's that, then, thought Earl, and he picked up the loafers and headed out to the beach. Though it was nearly dusk, the sun was still hot out there—the last rays of the day seemed to cut right through the jungle of palms and sea grapes to keep the beach heated. Still, the eastern horizon was beginning to darken and seemed to march toward him, swallowing up everything in its cool, deep blue. Soon, it would swallow him, too, and he'd be cool at last—his brow would no longer sweat and his eyes would no longer squint and his lungs would no longer feel the weight of the air. He'd be cool and light as ice.

First things first, though: Earl held the shoes up and looked at them one last time; no longer afraid to touch them, he rubbed them clean with his palm and looked at his soft brown reflection. Then he took a step toward the surf and threw them out into the thick green swells. He watched them as if he were watching his own fate. The waves pushed them down and smothered them, pulled them back up, and dragged them slowly out to sea with the tide. He watched until they were out of sight.

Earl felt a strange sense of relief, then. He knew the shoes had some sort of power over him, but he didn't know how much until he was finally rid of them. He laughed out loud at these superstitions. But the more he thought of it, the more he realized the feeling wasn't so crazy after all. He hadn't just convinced himself of the magical powers of the shoes, he'd convinced the whole town, save Mely. They'd all believed, just like he did, that the good fortune of the town was in some indescribable, almost unspeakable way connected to Earl's found pair of loafers. He could see that, now, when he remembered the way they'd always asked him about his shoes, the way they'd looked down at those shoes with awe and wonderment in their eyes, and maybe a little fear, too. But above all, faith. They'd never have said anything. It wasn't the kind of thing folks talk about. It was a feeling, though, passed from one to another without anybody ever having to speak. The shoes had a power beyond words.

Earl filled himself with the exhilaration of these thoughts, until he remembered he'd just tossed the shoes into the ocean.

Then he had to laugh again, to let the hot air out. He had to laugh at the way his thoughts lagged so fatally behind his actions.

He stepped into the lip of the surf and felt the water cooling his feet. He stepped deeper and deeper until the waves broke against his waist. His whole body was getting cool. It made him feel good, and he thought how funny it was that he was leaving here just the way he'd come almost a quarter century ago. He'd flung his hands away from the side of the SS *Seaworthy*'s lifeboat, trying to do then what he was going to do today. In that respect he'd be a success, at least. His tragic biography would show only how his continual failures served to provide him with the courage to finish what he should have finished on his very first day in Figulus. He'd been so full of energy and ideas then, and he'd tried so hard to make something for himself and for the town. He'd just lacked what it took. He wasn't destined for greatness after all, it looked like. He was another mediocre fella who'd tried and failed. If only he'd had something more unique, something that could bring people in from all over the country. The tropical wilderness and the beautiful beaches had not been enough. Nor had Mely's home cooking and the quaint little restaurant. If only he'd come up with something awe-inspiring, something that filled people with wonderment the way those shoes had affected the townsfolk. Or the way that Barefoot Mailman story had affected Elias Rathmartin.

It was then, with his shirt ballooning around his neck, and the water up to his dry and cracked lips, about to silence him forever, that Earl got an idea.

Chapter 21

WHEN HE TIED his boat up at the dock, Earl leapt out and began shouting.

"I seen 'im! I seen 'im! I seen the ghost!"

He ran up and down the little paths, past the post office, past the restaurant, past every little house in the community, throwing up his arms and shouting like some snake-kissing Baptist minister.

"I seen 'im! I been to the beach and I seen 'im!"

Slowly, the citizens emerged from their houses and from their goat- and pigpens, and from their little gardens, curious at any commotion outside of what they expected once a week from the Yankees.

Earl poked his head in his own house, too.

"I seen the ghost, Mely! You got to come and hear me out."

"What ghost, Earl?"

"The ghost that saved my life, Mely!"

She rose reluctantly from the rocker, pleased to see him in better spirits but not sure she was in the mood for one of Earl's tall tales. She followed him outside, and Earl lit the torches as people began to gather near the restaurant.

"What's wrong, Mayor Earl?"

"What's all yer fuss about?"

Earl stepped into their midst and began his testimony about the ghost.

"Listen now, ya don't have ta believe me, but ya ought to because it's the truth. Today, the mail come in and with it come my shoes, back from New York and polished finer'n I ever seen 'em. They did somethin to loosen 'em up, too, so they fit better'n ever. They fit so good, I thought I'd take 'em out to the beach for a little stroll, and Josh McCready was kind enough to loan me his boat for jes that purpose. Ain't that right, Josh?"

"It's so, Mayor Earl."

"An Mely, she seen me leave the house with them shoes. Weren't they lookin all shiny, Mely? An didn't ya ask me where I was goin, but I was too pleased and comf'table in my shoes ta pay ya any mind? Warn't that so, Mely? It was like my feet was bein massaged by the Hand of the Lord. Warn't that so, Mely?"

"Well I seen ya, Earl, sure enough. Ya floated right by without a word to me. But I don't know about no holy massage."

"See, you hear her—'floated right by.' I tell ya, I felt joy risin up from my feet, and I shoulda known somethin was gone ta happen. I shoulda known it right then."

"Well what in the darn hell happened, Earl?"

"I'll tell ya. I went out to the beach, taking Josh's skiff, just like he said, passin by the old Steinmetz place, you know, which is all broke down and burnt out and kinda spooky now. I got the creepiest feelin passin through there, and lookin back on it now, I shoulda known right then somethin was gone ta happen. But he caught me unawares, I tell ya. Completely unawares."

"Who caught ya, Mayor Earl? Tell us."

"It was a man all of ya know. Least, ya heard of 'im. An ya ain't likely ta b'lieve me when I tells ya, but ya ought to because it's the truth. I was walkin that beach, feelin comf'table as a pig in a poke—in m'shoes, ya know—when all at once I see this feller comin up from the south, comin up the beach

194

straight for me. Ya don't expect ta see no one on the beach, perticularly at sunset, and I reckon that shoulda told me somethin there, but I was blind, I tell ya, blind with comfort! Well, when he came up near on me, I saw what he looked like, and I begin to get a little scared."

"What'd he look like, Earl? Ya got to tell us, now!"

"He was all hunched over, like he had chains around his neck, or like he was some kind a ogre. He had a big purple nose, broken in three places, looked like. An two black, glowin eyes that seemed to look out at ya from another world—a world *beyond this one!*"

The crowd gasped. They'd all heard the ghost stories by now and immediately recognized a description of the Ghost of the Barefoot Mailman.

"Fact, his whole body seemed to glow. I noticed it then, but I didn't think nothin of it, because I was blind!"

"You *was* blind, Earl."

"I'd a known who that was straight off."

"Yer right, who wouldn't, and it's m'own fault that I didn't run. Fact is, he came right up to me, and I reached out my hand ta innerduce myself. That's when I first noticed his feet—they was all blistered up and bloody, like he'd been walkin for days and days out on that beach without nothin to cover his toes."

"That's him all right. That's the one!"

"I still warn't scared enough fer my own good, 'cause all at once I begin to feel sorry for 'im, he was in sech bad shape. So I said, 'Hey, feller, you need these shoes more'n I do,' and like the fool I am, and the fool y'all know I am, I took them fancy loafers right off my feet and handed them to 'im."

The crowd gasped again at Earl's foolishness, but also at his selflessness and bravery.

"His whole expression changed then. He looked at me real grateful, like it was the first thing anybody'd ever given 'im in his whole durned life. Then he took my hand and looked at me with them deep, black, glowin eyes, and said, in a hoarse, sorta whispery voice, 'You have saved me from eternal purgatory.'"

The small crowd began to mutter among themselves, clarifying to each other exactly what this meant.

"He left me then, headin north up the beach and wearin my best shoes, which I'd thought was gone ta be too big, but instead seemed to shrink around his feet and fit 'im perfeckly, like they was meant for 'im all along. It was only after he was out of sight did I realize what I'd done. Now, ya know I don't take no stock in ghost stories, and ya can ask our mail carrier if ya think I do—he's been tryin to fill me with ghost stories ever since he took the job, and I turn 'im a deaf ear ever time. But folks, it was jes that deaf ear that made me blind to what was happenin to me out there on the beach. 'Cause sure enough, this man fit the ticket, and I suddenly realized I'd given my shoes TO THE GHOST OF THE BARE-FOOT MAILMAN!!"

Now the whole crowd (except for Mely) oohed and aahed and closed in to shake Earl's hand, the same hand that had touched a ghost. And after they'd shook it, they inspected their own hands to see if something had rubbed off. They asked each other, "Did you feel that, too?" and agreed that there was some kind of slippery spark that passed off him, that the postmaster must have received some small bit of otherworldly power from touching the ghost.

Several folks took him aside and asked him to repeat the story, which he did happily. Then several more took him into their homes, poured him some whiskey, and prodded him for more details, which he was all too happy to give, embellishing here and there, and eventually giving them the impression he'd held a regular interview with the ghost concerning such subjects as God and the afterlife and a few of the acquaintances the ghost had met since he'd died, which happened to include deceased relatives of some of the townsfolk.

The whole town was abuzz with Earl's news, and the people who didn't get a chance to quiz Earl quizzed each other about Earl's story, themselves embellishing and extrapolating a little, which they figured was okay as long as they maintained the spirit of the story, though some of them objected to this liberty-taking and began to argue over a few of the minor details—

". . . and like the devil hisself, his eyes were glowin bright red—"

"Yella, I tell ya! Yella! He warn't from hell, he was from purgatory, and everbody knows the color of purgatory is yella!"

"It's his skin was yella. A ghost's eyes always glow red, no matter he's in purgatory or hell. I know, cause I seen 'em before."

"Well I seen this one, jes last week, and I tell ya his eyes was yella!"

"You done no sech thing, and them's fightin words—!"

But all in all, people were pretty pleased with the event and agreed it was a sign that great things were in store for their little town, that from now on the place was blessed by a guardian angel, that now they had a friend in a high place who was eternally grateful for Earl's small gesture of kindness. They praised Earl for this kindness and for his bravery, and they praised themselves for putting up with Earl's big talk all these years.

Earl spent a splendid evening basking in the limelight. Somebody tuned up a fiddle, and Earl grabbed his wife and danced like he was nineteen again. Mely had shaken her head at Earl's story, but his energy and his youthfulness were affecting and got her right in her soft spot. They both were drunk with vitality, hope, and alcohol, and they danced until late in the night.

When it was finally over, though, Earl wasn't too drunk to light a candle at his desk and tell his story once more, this time in writing. He told the complete and unabridged version, with every embellishment he could remember from the whole beautiful evening, at least the embellishments that didn't conflict with other embellishments. And when he'd finished, he folded up the letter and stuck it in an envelope he addressed to John Thomas, reporter for the *New York Times*. Then he felt a hand on his shoulder and turned in his chair to face his wife.

"Earl," she said. "Come ta bed now." She wasn't too drunk, either.

Chapter 22

WHEN JOHN THOMAS received the letter from the postmaster of Figulus, he was putting the finishing touches on his book tentatively titled: *Barefoot Mailman: The Life and Times of an American Legend*. He had expanded his five-part *Times* piece into five hundred manuscript pages, giving finer and finer detail about both the history of the Mailman himself and Thomas's travels with him. As the book evolved, Thomas also found it necessary to shape the story's meaning for a public that seemed curiously attracted to the shoeless figure. He found himself digressing into long discursive passages that commented on the man as a symbolic figure for a hero-starved American public, and then digressing even further into an analysis of the public's need for legends and myths. Thus the book became not just a biography but also a diagnostic summary of the American psyche, its unfulfilled needs and displaced desires, where it was going and where it had been. The total effect was an indictment of the bourgeois status quo that had stagnated the great American Dream: it took a figure like the Barefoot Mailman, rising from the lowest rungs of society, to show Americans that their fate was still in their own hands.

In the afternoon haze of his woody mid-town apartment, John Thomas read Earl Shank's letter with great interest.

He had no way of determining the ghost story's validity, of course, but it intrigued him nonetheless because it solved a nagging problem in his book, a problem that had caused him to overflow his wastebasket with crumpled paper, cover his desktop with scribbled notes of not-quite-adequate ideas, and make an unprecedented number of trips to the tobacco shop to keep his pipe filled as he thought. As it stood, his final chapter concluded with the Mailman's reported disappearance (a report brought back by Southwind cruise passengers), and this raised the destructive possibility that the man had either given up or been fired by some postmaster too embarrassed to admit it now. These possibilities were interesting in an ironical sort of way, Thomas had to admit, but they would spell doom for the legend and thus for Thomas's chances to parlay it into everlasting acknowledgment of his genius.

He couldn't let that happen; this was his baby, and it had to be nurtured. Now comes this ghost story providing some evidence, no matter how flimsy, that the man had, in fact, died, and that the torment and alienation that drove him through life had continued to drive him even after death, until one man—this cracker postmaster—finally showed him a little compassion. John Thomas recognized this as the best possible conclusion for his book. Even if it was a bit far-fetched, he could just stick it in there and let the readers decide for themselves. He knew which way they'd decide, because he knew how much they wanted this legend to survive, and he knew also that the best security for any legend is the death of the man who fostered it.

A few months later, when the book was published, the final chapter created a stir since the author and the publisher had kept it secret right up until the publication date. The legend, of course, was well known by now, but this ghost story seemed to add a different texture, providing a mysterious yet satisfactory closure to the mailman's tragic tale. And the book as a whole stirred up the American people, who ceased to be jaded and cynical when they thought of the plight of the

Barefoot Mailman, and who felt, at least for a while, they could make a difference after all. Many politicians lost their jobs that year, and the American people again seized the reigns of destiny.

IN FIGULUS, TIME seemed to grind to a halt without the weekly visitation of Yankees. People had been so used to the excitement of Tuesdays, and the quick and easy money, that when the ships stopped coming, they didn't know what to do with themselves. Earl's ghost story created some excitement for them and gave them a rich topic for conversation, but when Tuesday came and went without one sale of an embroidered wallhanging saying "Bless This House" or a whittled and painted figure of a pink curlew or a Florida panther, and without a single guest for Earl's restaurant, people got pretty bored and depressed. They made an effort to recreate their former lives; after all, they'd already made more money than they'd ever need in Figulus. But as they went through the motions, something was missing. They'd tasted the fruit of the Yankee dollar, and that was a taste they could not forget.

They sweated through the summer. The air was heavy, and no matter how little they ate, their bodies seemed to weigh too much for this earth. They didn't speak much, and when they worked, they didn't get much done. Everyone prayed for a change of weather, or another ghost story, something to shake things up and take their minds off what now seemed inevitable—that they'd never see another boatload of slumming Yankees again.

For Earl, the air was heavy, too, but with expectation. He was certain that something was astir up north that would have great repercussions in their little town. He was happy and hopeful, and no one could figure out why. He hadn't told anyone of the letter from the Rathmartin boys, not even Mely, and he hadn't told anyone of his letter to John Thomas. When people asked him why he was in such a good mood all the time, seeing as how he wasn't getting any business these days, he'd reply that it was just the off-season, and he was going to relax and enjoy his off-season, because when the boats came in again in the fall, it was going to be nothing but work.

People didn't say anything because they didn't want to burst his bubble. They just looked at each other, and in that look was the confirmation that Earl had finally lost his mind, that the touch of a ghost was too much for any mortal to bear, that Earl was showing the symptoms of his exposure to the Beyond, and that it was probably for the best, since the shock of another lost dream would be too much for him to bear, anyway. Even Mely was afraid of what was going to happen in the fall when the cruise ships didn't show up and Earl stood waiting on the dock with his big hand outstretched and his jaw muscles beginning to give way under the weight of an unreturned smile.

Earl didn't see how people looked at him with pity. He saw only what was going to happen when his story had made its way into the proper channels and business returned better than ever. He spent much of his days in the restaurant, keeping it clean and fixing it up, and when he couldn't think of anything to fix, he'd row himself across the lake and spend a little time on the beach, not the least bit bothered by the sun as he walked in the sand and relived his now-famous encounter with the ghost.

It was on one of these afternoon walks, in late September, that he spotted a ship coming from the north. He watched it grow on the horizon, slowly moving just inside the Gulf Stream until it stopped at the inlet, just a few miles up the coast.

He paddled his skiff back to town and ran the length of it, screaming, "I tole ya! I tole ya! The Yankees've come again! I seen 'em, and they've come again!"

Everyone was shocked, and they made quick preparations, though they all figured it was poor Earl's mind gone astray for good, that this was just the beginning of a lot of false alarms stemming from Earl's hallucinations. Still, most of them set up their craft stands and pulled out all the leftover knick-knacks, because with something like this it was better to be safe than sorry. Earl even got Mely to fire up something in the kitchen, though she did it with tears in her eyes, thinking she was only doing it to soothe Earl's deeply troubled mind.

But sure enough, when the Southwind tender pulled up to the dock, the whole town sent up a cheer, and Earl's hand was shaken heartily and his smile was returned eagerly by two well-dressed men who turned out to be the Rathmartin boys, come personally to offer their apologies to the entire town, and to present Earl with a generous new contract.

The Rathmartins stayed to dinner, and when they'd eaten all the gator they could handle and bought all the crafts they could carry, they posed for pictures taken by a *Times* photographer they'd brought along just for that purpose. Poof! Like magic, there was Earl signing the contract. There was Earl shaking the hand of Stanislaw, then shaking the hand of Merwyn. There was Earl hugging his wife, and Earl standing outside his restaurant, torches burning and eyes aglow, a smile as big as Florida, and the whole town looking on with a mixture of awe and pride, like they'd just discovered him in their midst as a man whose dreams were as good as a promise.

Chapter 23

T HREE YEARS LATER, Earl's restaurant had lived up to all his expectations. Not only did he have regular business from Southwind Cruise Lines—now twice a week—but also from four other cruise lines as well. Figulus became a standard port of call for southbound passenger ships. Everyone was getting richer and richer. Earl had to expand the restaurant more than once, extending it further and further into the Florida wilderness, so that it came to resemble a long, low barn, with a seating capacity of one hundred fifteen rich Yankees. The walls were decorated with sailing pictures and with the arts and crafts of the locals, all with small price tags attached. The path from the dock to the restaurant had been widened, and all the arts-and-crafts booths had been joined together under a single roof, so that even when it was raining the cruise ship passengers could fondle and inspect the local products at their leisure. But the most important artifact in town was something Earl had ordered from New York, built to his detailed specifications: an exact replica of the loafers that had made him famous, on display just inside the entrance to his restaurant.

After the publication of John Thomas's book, Earl had won instant fame, particularly among the wealthy and highbrow circles of New York and the greater Northeast. For many, Earl and his restaurant became attraction enough to make a trip to Florida worthwhile. They came to taste the specialty of the house—fried gatortail (now cooked in small chunks to hide its reptilian features), and to hear Earl tell stories—particularly the one of his famous meeting with the ghost. But perhaps most of all they came to see, to touch, and to look at their reflections in the perfect leather reconstruction of the shoes that had ascended to the Hereafter on the feet of the Barefoot Mailman.

It was this replica that so startled a young Brooklynite one December evening, when, helped by his wife, he hobbled into Earl's restaurant at the end of a line of Southwind cruise guests.

JOSEF STEINMETZ HAD been happily reunited with his wife when he'd left Florida four years before. He'd spent several weeks in the hospital undergoing treatment for exposure, and another few months recovering at home with his Lena and his Aunt Lois by his side. His feet were scarred and oversensitive from the experience and would be always. His doctor gave him therapeutic boots to wear, but they were of little comfort, so he still required help walking on uneven or soft surfaces and took a cane wherever he went.

Worse yet were his mental scars. He refused to discuss, even with Lena (especially with Lena!), any of the terrible events that had taken place just before his departure from Florida. He resigned himself to living with his private shame, and that meant living a lie. Lena never suspected his infidelity, but the hypocrisy took its toll on Josef—on his self-esteem and his health.

Though he could not heal his mental scars, he quickly became obsessed with finding comfort for his sad feet, and spent long hours studying the latest developments in shoemaking techniques and applying them with little success in the room he'd converted into a workshop. These efforts had led to something practical for him. The family print shop having been sold, he'd opened a cobbler's shop on one of the famed Brooklyn avenues with the small sum of money left to him by his Uncle Mordy. This shop came to have a solid reputation and was moderately successful in a short time. He made enough money to sustain himself, his wife, and his aunt, but not enough to enjoy the simple luxuries they'd all been accustomed to while Mordy was alive. And none of his shoemaking innovations had yet provided him with any luxury for his feet.

On weekends, he occasionally read books for pleasure, but they were mainly books on shoemaking. He remained enclosed in this small world and never once came across a reference to the story he'd given birth to in the mind of the *New York Times* reporter.

He tried his best to forget his experiences in Florida, but he didn't always have the strength of will to do so, and when he fell into despair and self-pity, he permitted himself this one indulgence: he would ask his dear Aunt Lois to describe for him down to the minutest detail everything she knew about the loafers his Uncle Mordy had sent him from his death bed. "Dear Lois," he'd say, "tell me again about the shoes," and she did so gladly and often, because she knew that the story would soothe Josef's emotional scars, and because she never passed up an opportunity to speak about Mordy's great kindness and generosity.

So, because Josef had an exact image of those loafers etched onto his brain, he was in for a wrenchingly unpleasant surprise when he found the replicas—of the same brand and matching in every detail the shoes his uncle had addressed to him years earlier—just inside the door of Postmaster General's.

He had returned to Florida on the advice of his new doctor, the latest in a long series of doctors he'd employed for his foot ailments. All of them had been useless, but this one took a holistic approach, claiming that there was no physical reason for his persistent foot pain, that the symptoms pointed toward something psychosomatic. When Josef—out of desperation—finally told him the origins of his foot problems, the doctor recommended that he return to the scene of his mental anguish and slay those demons that seemed to haunt his poor feet. So, with the help of Aunt Lois's small savings, Josef boarded a Southwind liner with his wife and made the journey south, with nervous trepidation and a sweat that never left his brow. His feet quaked in their therapeutic boots, and Lena tried to comfort him as he lay feverish in his cabin.

Nevertheless, when the ship reached the inlet, he gathered his resolve and boarded the tender, knowing he had to do it—for himself and, more importantly, for the memory of his dear uncle. He couldn't live the rest of his life in fear and shame and the constant pain that had taken root in his weak mind. If he could face up to his failures maybe one day he could tell Lena the truth.

Everything seemed to be going fine until he stepped through that door and saw the shoes, glued to a sort of lectern with an engraved caption:

THE SHOES THAT SAVED

THE BAREFOOT MAILMAN

FROM ETERNAL PURGATORY

*(If you don't know the story, ask me,
Earl Shank,
the man who gave them to the ghost.)*

Josef's feet failed him completely, then, and his wife tried to catch him, but she succeeded only in cushioning his fall. When Earl rushed over to see what was the matter, he found himself looking into the glazed, swollen, and prematurely aged eyes of his long-lost mail carrier.

Right away, Earl sensed the danger this man posed to his livelihood. If any of these tourists knew Josef Steinmetz's sad story, if any of the townsfolk recognized him, Postmaster General's might be lost for good, and Earl Shank's reputation would float down river and sink once and for all. This was an event that could tastefully be omitted from his memoirs; it was a memory that would martyr itself for the sake of the legend. But later, whenever he thought about it, he'd think what a shame it was that the world would never know how quickly and skillfully he'd acted when the pressure was on.

He pulled the dazed and nearly limp immigrant to his feet and practically carried him out the door into the semi-darkness. He held him up by the shoulders.

"Mr. Steinmetz!" he said. "Yessir, it sure is a surprise to see you."

"Postmaster," said Josef, still stammering and gasping for breath. "Forgive me. Returning here is evidently too much for my faculties. I am seeing things—images of shoes and strange words—I'm afraid I've made a terrible mistake."

"Well, you sure did pull somethin over on all a'us. We thought you was dead and gone—eaten by gators, maybe, or shriveled up by the sun. An look at ya—here ya are!"

"I know I have no right to come here as a guest. I broke the solemn trust that you placed in me and failed this town as I have failed myself and my family." Josef tried to catch his breath. "I regret I don't have the resources for monetary compensation, but if it is required, I am prepared now to serve out whatever jail term you feel is appropriate."

The postmaster let go of Josef's shoulders now. "Ya oughtn't t'be so hard on yerself, Mr. Steinmetz. What ya done is yer own business. Listen, I don't know what ya done out there with the mail, but I don't reckon I care now. Everthing's worked out here jes fine, and as fer you, ya done more t'help than ya'll ever know."

Josef began to recover himself and bowed just slightly. "I thank you for your kind words," he said.

"They ain't jes words. Look," said Earl, taking Josef's arm and pulling him a little farther away from the restaurant.

"Maybe ya don't know it, but I'm gonna do ya a favor and tell ya somethin because ya don't deserve to spend the rest of yer life thinkin ya been beat. I don't know the perticulers, but somehow ya done a good thing for me and this town. Maybe ya didn't mean to, but ya helped make this place into a reg'lar paradise for all of us, and we owe ya a deep debt of gratitude, though most of us don't even know that much. It's a funny thing that a feller can create such an impression merely by showin his face once or twice, and a funnier thing still that he kin become more famous after he's gone than he could ever hope to be while he's still around. I reckon people like to make somethin out of nothin more'n they like to make some-thin out of somethin else. But my point is, Mr. Steinmetz, I got a personal debt to you, and I aim to pay it—on one con-dition, though—ya don't never tell yer story to nobody—I mean, don't talk about yer missin shoes or yer days workin for the U.S. Postal Service. That could ruin me, never mind how. An it wouldn't help you any, neither, cause what I'm proposin right now is to give ya a fair ten percent of my profits here. Ten percent, and ya ain't got to do nothin for it—jes set back in yer home up north, keep quiet about it, and col-lect a monthly check from me. Consider it a small token of my gratitude for what kin never be repaid. How bout it, Mr. Steinmetz?"

"Postmaster, I'm baffled by your talk. If you ask me not to talk about my shoes or my experiences here, you have no need—these memories weigh on my chest daily. They are too painful to speak of. And if ever I think about them too long, my feet begin to throb and remind me of the completeness of my failure. I failed through my own foolishness and am owed no pity or profits."

"Then think of it as a business deal, Mr. Steinmetz. You don't know it, but you helped make this restaurant a success—and of course I had a part in it too, with my publicity skills, ya understand. So I'm makin you ten percent owner, and ya don't even have to help run the place. In fact, it'd be better if ya didn't show up at all. Jes stay at home and take care a them beautiful golden feet a yers."

Earl held out his hand. Josef was about to refuse it, then he remembered his wife. With the extra money, he could take her to the theater and to dinner, and he could buy her the fancy dresses and parasols she deserved, to promenade up and down the grand Brooklyn boulevards. He could give Lena the life she'd expected when he'd first proposed to her, and he could give his Aunt Lois some semblance of the quality of life she'd had with Mordy. He could not accept the money for himself because he was an unworthy and unfaithful failure, but he would accept it for them, and for the child Lena now held within her, and for the children and the grandchildren to come. Of course, in accepting the postmaster's offer, he'd never be able to tell Lena the truth about what happened on his mail route, but under the circumstances, he decided he could live with that, as he had for the past three years. The selfish lie would become a selfless one, or would at least have a selfless component.

"Postmaster, though I am unworthy, I will accept your offer if it pleases you."

They shook on it, and as they did, Josef noticed over the postmaster's shoulder the shape of the renovated restaurant, and how strangely similar it was to the long, low winery back in Melk that his dear Uncle Mordy had so skillfully rendered into a towering convent on a cliff, with the Donau running below it. He realized how deeply that image was etched into him, and how closely connected to his uncle, so that it almost seemed like Mordy himself on the cliff, in all his majesty and kindness, looking down on him and smiling on those lives that still flowed beneath him and loved him. In that moment, Josef forgot completely about the loafers he'd once desired so badly, and his heart filled with the simple knowledge of being loved.

Earl was greatly relieved at these events and sighed through his toothy grin. He invited Josef to dine, but made him promise to turn away should any of the townsfolk wander in. It would be too risky if one of them should recognize him.

They re-entered the restaurant, and Josef walked right past the displayed loafers without even a glance at them. Things had settled into the usual routine. Mely had helped up Mrs. Steinmetz and showed her to her table, where they'd had a short talk to catch up on things. Mely was glad to see them, though she wasn't all that surprised. She'd never fully believed Earl's ghost stories. She'd just let him indulge himself.

All went well with dinner until Earl began to clear the plates, and then a man walked in, screaming, "I'll murder every damn Yankee in here!!"

Everything silenced, and Earl dropped a stack of dishes. There was the old rebel mail carrier, now with a long beard, but still in the same old tattered clothes, and still with the same fermented smell about him.

The guests—all but the Steinmetzes, that is, who thought they were reliving a horrible nightmare—quickly figured this man to be a part of the entertainment. They watched him with smiles on their faces—now they were going to be shown what the real South was like, the South they'd only read about in books, full of foul-smelling, Yankee-hating rebels and dainty Southern belles; they fully expected a dame in a hoop skirt to come through the door next, and for a chivalrous plantation owner to rescue her from this dirty man's clutches.

Instead, though, the old mail carrier marched through the tables, knocking off plates and pushing over empty chairs until he came to the Steinmetz table. He put his knuckles down on it and leered at Josef with narrow eyes.

"I know you," he said. "I blackened yer eyes once and I'll do it again, by God. I been up and down this coast and I know yer whole story. Ya may've fooled the Injuns—their tribe's split up and they've all took hotel jobs down in Biscayne, believin they're white now. And ya may've fooled them beach scavengers—enough to send one a their men to his drownin death. And ya may've fooled that fool Yankee reporter and give him a story to write. But ya ain't fooled me! Yer a fraud, mister, and I aim to expose ya once and fer all!"

And with that, he turned around to address the restaurant crowd and expose the big fraud that had been pulled on all of them. But as he did so, he came face to face with the thick, fleshy knuckles of Earl Shank.

When the reb fell to the floor, hitting his head on the Steinmetz's table, the whole restaurant rose to its feet and gave Earl a standing ovation.

"Marvelous show!"

"So realistic!"

"I heard a noise—it sounded like he really hit him!"

"Unbelievable!"

"This is the real McCoy. The stuff you don't find in books!"

"Somebody ought to write one!"

"And our host—what an actor! That man's gonna be famous one day."

"Handsome devil, too!"

"A man like that has a future in state politics, I say."

Earl took his bow that night, as he did every night from then on, though that was the only time he threw the punch. He tracked down and hired China, the Indian guide, to come in and throw the punch for him, because she'd seemed to enjoy so much hitting the reb that first time, when Rathmartin and his doctor were present. And China, who'd felt the only real satisfaction in her life when she threw that punch at the white man's face, found it difficult to refuse the job. She was paid a generous salary to come in nightly and punch the lights out of the drunken mail carrier, who got so drunk every night he'd forget he'd just been punched out the night before. When he did remember and stayed away from the restaurant, Earl had Josh McCready on call to come in and act the part. When that happened, no real punches were supposed to be thrown, but sometimes China couldn't resist, and then Earl would have to pay Josh something extra for combat duty. Each night, when the punch-out was over and the man was dragged out by his feet, Earl gave a little speech about the constant battle that raged in Florida between civilization and the untamed wilds. Sometimes the jungle creeped into a man's head and took control of his actions, but there were always men like himself who bore the torch of civilization, and personally, he was confident that civilization would win in the end and we'd tame the wilds, just like we'd tame the beasts within ourselves. Then he bowed, basking in the round of heartfelt applause, applause that he seemed to hear constantly now, a sort of background noise in his head.

For China, it was a bitter event. She heard Earl's speech and it enraged her the way he glorified his people, the same people who'd massacred her tribe. But even more it enraged her because she knew he was right—that his civilization was going to win out in the end and there was nothing she could do about it anymore. They were coming in droves now, far faster than she could ever hope to escort out. There were hotels being built on the beaches just to the north, and a railroad line had already extended its steel grip as far south as Fort Pierce. Soon it would pass through here, and its churning locomotive and its multitudes of tourists, settlers, and fortune-seekers would wipe clean and purify any regrets that civilization might have had about what it had done to her people. So she resigned herself to the one last thing on this earth that could give her any pleasure: to punch a white man nightly in the face.

Epilogue

APRIL 2, 1894, WAS a windy day. Elias Rathmartin was sailing the Atlantic in search of mermaids, having commandeered an old sailing ship from his company. He was getting very old and, the crew said, senile. His mind slipped into such distant imaginings that at times he thought himself a merman who'd somehow been changed into a human—he told his crew that he'd been transformed at an early age and sent among the bipeds to make contact and teach them the ways of the mer-people. The problem was, he'd forgotten their customs, or hadn't learned them well enough—after all, he'd been only a tyke when he'd left the sea. So now, he said, it was more important than ever that he find one of his mer-friends and relearn their ways.

He spent long hours in the crow's nest, eyes peeled for the tell-tale splash of a mermaid's tail. On this day he did spot something—but something only a demented mind could truly believe was a mermaid. In a fit of crazed ecstasy, he leapt from the top of the crow's nest, yelling his merman's call and believing that he was at last going to rejoin his kind, that he had only to open his arms and embrace the mother ocean to return to his watery paradise. The crew looked up in horror when they heard him yell, and they followed his graceful swan dive through the beautiful blue sky, all the way down to

214

the mid-ship deck. There was at least someone, however—perhaps a man with some romantic notions himself, a man who thought that just maybe there was the slimmest of possibilities that the admiral was right—who looked not at the admiral's fall, but at where the admiral's eyes had been fixed. As the admiral made his final descent, the man took a step to the ship's rail and spotted, fifty yards off starboard, what looked like a pair of leather shoes, bobbing in the waves with little splashes that seemed mischievous and beckoning.

The crew prepared to ice Elias Rathmartin's body and return it to his family. But before a makeshift casket could be built, the ship ran up against a strong gale and murderous seas. In the scramble, the crew forgot about their boss's body until it was spotted sliding toward the stern, whereupon it was flipped into the consuming waves. It was a burial at sea, performed by the sea herself, and it was exactly how Elias Rathmartin would have wanted it.

When it was all over and the crew had stopped blaming each other and themselves, they agreed that it was really the proper way, and that just maybe the old admiral hadn't gone so crazy after all, that maybe he did belong to the depths, and that when the sea calls back one of her own, she's going to get him, one way or another.

This was the last recorded sighting of Josef Steinmetz's famous loafers, and signaled the beginning of the end of the Barefoot Mailman legend. John Thomas continued to write about it, but found the public's attention span remarkably short and its loyalty to its heroes remarkably tenuous. His readership declined rapidly, and reviewers and critics accused him of beating a dead horse. When he could no longer find a publisher, and when all of his business investments went under, he was forced to take a job as the editor of *The Barefoot Daily: News to Kick Your Shoes Off By*, the shipboard newspaper of the Southwind Cruise Lines. He was a bitter man, eventually fired from even this job because of his sour and unsuitable editorials.

The Steinmetz loafers never did reach their intended destination, of course. Let loose in the sea, it seems probable that they've gotten caught up in the current of the Gulf Stream, and, floating on their soles and slashing through waves, continue to circle the Atlantic like a pair of beckoning mermaids or sharks on the prowl.